VALLEY OF DEADLY SHADOWS

A FANTASY NOVELLA

JONATHAN EVAN HUDSON

VALLEY OF DEADLY SHADOWS

CHAPTER

ONE

The sky was a cherry custard for the eyes. The clouds, wisps of white chocolate pudding, the best kind of chocolate pudding. The sun, the perfect dash of cherry on top.

And a sunset on mankind if Roo failed this crazy mission.

It was just one of those missions a guy needed to see the sweet side of things whenever possible.

Like the pyramid in the distance.

It gleamed so bright with its sides plated in such lush gold any thief — guy or girl — would give their left ball for the chance to loot it down to its foundation of marble white bone.

Never mind how each level was molded like a sinister pearl-themed grimoire full of pearly skulls, pearl-crusted horns, and other gothic pearl-coated creepiness.

Never mind how the gold reflected the sunlight.

As in it was shining *black*, and not just any black, but black as the Abysmal Void all demons came from. Not whitish yellow, you know, like a noon sun.

Like actual normal *precious* gold.

Even weirder, the black was lined with a hint of bright pink you only saw in the sky before a massive hellhole of a thunderstorm.

The tingle down his spine, so freezing compared to the steam bath of stagnant air that, well, it was already so hot a pair of briefs was overdressing, so a chill even from a bit of fear, a nice relief.

If the reason behind it wasn't so dire.

And the reason no sensible guy would forsake his dragon scale here. His jerkin, his trousers — even his cowled sleeved cloak, and gloves — all pale blue dragon scale that could deflect worldly and otherworldly fang and claw, steel blade and magicked blade, just like any decent dragon scale. Even his suede boots had dragon scale sewed and glued on.

Including the soles.

Good thing too.

The ground here was slippier than a tavern's floor during All Summer's Eve festival (only a few more weeks away too! And the best reason to hurry saving mankind.)

A hollow howl echoed throughout the valley.

Not exactly wolfish either.

More like a gut-cringing warning of the unspeakable horrors eager to haunt and hunt in this world.

It was almost, *almost* enough to blame the moss sliming this outcrop of lumpy boulders and be done with it. It made this cliff smoother and slicker than Prince Sieg going Tall, Dark, and Handsome for their latest lustdream-come-true elf maiden companion while combing his blond spiky hairdo spikier for the zillionth time.

(Why was he combing his hair out here in the ass end of nowhere? Especially after that horrifying howl. He's a prince. Why not?)

But that latest lustdream-come-true elf maiden was still down in that valley, leaping around like a grasshopper all liquored up on vodkaed daiquiri.

She hopped branch to branch through the thick forest. Scouted out the area ahead. Looking for a way mere humans could crawl down the cliff.

And ... honestly, even from a thousand feet up, those oaks she was no doubt hopping through looked a lot like giant woodified spiderwebs thick with leafy toupees.

Her outfit was similar to Roo's blue dragon scale and Sieg's gold-as-his-hair dragon scale — except hers was green dragon scale and far more form-fitting.

(And what elf didn't wear green everything?)

It made it hard to spot her from way up here too.

It might be her leaping back toward the cliff.

It might be orcs in a mottled green.

All True TriCross Knights had the emblems of tricrosses embedded point first in angelically winged stone nowadays, so civilians and allies could identify them.

Also enemies could impersonate them but details details.

Just in case of an orc encounter, Roo fingered his revolver crossbow. It was a hand sized revolver. A seven-chamber automatic. Normally, it could only hit something within a few dozen yards, but the extra height here should be enough to reach any trouble down below.

If he was willing to reveal their positions, that was.

A few quiet flaps and a crow landed on Roo's shoulder.

That familiar weight ... Razz. Good.

Razz was a talking crow and Roo's truest partner in this mess for over a decade since his original, long lost home was annihilated by some nightmarish Light-knows-what freaks.

(Never mind what happened to his second home ... but not all elves went psycho. Just ... too many.)

The same time Razz lost his entire flock to the same dark horror.

Time to face down another horror together.

And do more than just survive this time.

Time flies when waiting for orcs to appear.

The cherry sky didn't show any serpents flying their way, so thank the Light for small favors. Friendly dragons were far and few in between, but this dragon scale wasn't from hostile dragons.

No, it was a gift. Skin shed by allied dragons.

The wispy clouds like white chocolate hadn't attracted any sky sirens, basically mermaids of the sky and wow, if only those mermaids weren't skin deep beauties but I digress ...

Because the cherry sun could easily attract a dark phoenix and those flame-loving birds were nearly immortal, and a bitch to take down.

Almost as bad as a hostile dragon.

Almost.

The forest with its twisty long-branched trees with their leafy toupees was no doubt full of tree trolls — basically trolls in the form of trees, demented in mind and body, and nasty all around, but hard as hell to kill.

But those branches were like giant cobwebbed spiderwebs in the form of thick wood.

Roo never saw a tree troll with such a shape.

Now lycan were technically beast trolls who evolved the ability to shift into human and elven counterparts and worse, the females had amazing regeneration, till they got staked.

Then they didn't even always die right away.

But those howls were no doubt wolf trolls. (Probably.) They always hunted in packs, and those wolf trolls were demented mind and body, if only their females were as demented in body but no.

The females were often as lovely as the elf girls they loved to munch.

(Something even his own mom, so that good bit of tigress blood in her, did her best to hide — until some elf maidens decided to go battle bitch against a young and vulnerable Roo.)

So trying to tell which of the green cloaked figures hopping down around those branches so far away, not with mere human eyes, and yes, their females were tigresses, usually, so the female lycan could easily hop between branches, and yes, they could hop even better than an elf girl playing grasshopper.

But Roo was reluctant to get any closer.

So far.

The slime on these boulders he was standing on, he trusted the dragon scale on his soles only so much, and that was more than the Tall, Dark, and Handsome Prince Sieg a decent bit behind him and still combing his hair of all things ...

At least Razz was settling into Roo's hair. Roo styled his own hair like a crow's nest, so it would be perfect for Razz, and a quiet caw let Roo know Razz was settled and ready for action.

More like chit chat but ...

"Baaad news," Razz said, "No way down."

"Except one," Roo said.

"A thoooousand foot fall?" Razz said, "Not even your hedgie powers would save you, and I go big for only a few moments. Not enough. Sorry sorry."

Ah, they were both hedgies. Short for hedge wizard. As in able to use a magical trick or two, called Hedges, compared to a wizard who could use lots of magic called spells and with much less limitations, but hedgie or wizard, magic always carried three limitations paired with a weakness, and it had to be connected to the nature of the power.

Also hexes worked too much like paper-rocks-scissors too often.

So rely too much on a single hex and you were bound to encounter the wrong hedgie and puff. Dead.

Unlike most hedgies and wizards, even Razz and Sieg, Roo focused on upping his core abilities to the max.

Hexes for him, just a fall back.

Razz could only go extra big and powerful for a short time. After a warm up period, the first limitation. The limited duration of the ability, the second limitation. Third limitation

was the cool down until he could use it again. The weakness.
the terrible exhaustion afterwards.

Simple limitations were best. Fail to respect limitation
and failing to cast the hex was the best you could hope for.

A nasty backlash more likely.

Core abilities, on the other hand, slow to build up like any
other natural ability that took training, but it was reliable.
Not exactly limited.

Throw in good technique and ...

(But his special Vorshaya bloodline, along with training
since his childhood, secret training for most of it, core abilities the best way to up those three major abilities to the max.)

(But to go to the next step ... even his scholarly mother
wasn't all too sure. Most of his clan was gone, so no one to
ask either, and the secret manuals in his pouch only revealed
so much ...)

No matter. He'd figure it out.

Now time to push Sieg to do the right thing.

"Hairdo Prince," Roo said, "Can your asspad cut some
stairs into this cliff?"

The asspad of a sword choked and stuttered from underneath Prince Sieg's ass.

"I. am. NOT. an. *asspad*," said the sword, "I am the one
and *only* Demon Ender, destroyer of demonkind, slayer of
darkling ilk everywhere—"

"Are-are-aren't demons and daaarklings the same thing?"
Razz said.

"Yes," said Demon Ender, "But—"

Roo scratched his (unfortunately) beardless chin.

"Ooooh," Roo said, "That's why your fluffy snow vixen sheath has Demon Ender in golden bubbly snow vixen hair on one side and Darkling Ender in lush blond snow vixen hair on the other side, right?"

"Um, yes," said Demon Ender, "I mean *yes!* Glad to know your eyes actually work. That viciously sly snow vixen—"

"Staaaake fodder?" Razz said, "Wolves guy lycan. Tigresses girl lycan. Snow vixen perverted girl lycan of the rare type. You like?"

"What?" said Demon Ender, "NO! All darklings—"

"No wonder Sieg is so silent," Roo said, "Pondering how to reunite with his snow vixen sexy who donated her pelt to his knife's sheath. Poor bitch regenerated but the pain, oh, the pain ..."

Sieg chuckled. "Don't underestimate vixens."

"Especially vixen witches?" Roo said, "Yeah yeah. Riiiight."

Sieg chuckled again.

"Underestimate them at your peril," Sieg said, "They're often stupid from their slavomancers inbreeding them, yes, but often incredibly sly. And stupid does the most unexpected things no expert could predict, so your steel stakes on your pouch, keep them close, Rowan. There's lycan coming to lead those orcs below."

Ugh. Roo loathed when Sieg used his given name.

But he refused to show it.

"Aye," Roo said, "But getting down there ..."

Roo squinted down the cliff. "Leena shouldn't be left to clear them all out herself."

There was definitely more than just one green cloaked slender down there jumping about the spiderweb of oaks and firing arrows art each other. Which one was Leena the lust-dream-come-true ... too far away to tell which was dragon scale and which was leather.

"She's a knight and an elf," Sieg said, "She can do it. Just like either of us can. Trust her. I know you only lust for her ..."

"Like you don't," Roo said.

"But I'll get to bed her soon enough," Sieg said, "You've never bedded any ... sigh, father warned me not to tease my lessers. Merely pity them for the troubles they'd have, troubles that I'd never truly understand myself, sigh, but as your Prince, I must try, as hard as it may be."

Razz cawed softly. "Tryyyyyy haaaaarder. Haaaarder. Haaarder than your trouser blade. Haaarder than—"

"Wait!" Roo said, "Look there."

CHAPTER

THREE

Roo pointed down the cliff for emphasis.

Among the spiderweb of oaks, through the thick of leaved toupees, a shapely green cloaked and cowled figure had lost the other three green, hopping figures. Put quite a bit of distance between them.

And settled down.

But now there were three more figures sneaking up on the shapely figure.

But those three figures, not cloaked in green, no.

They were —squint squint — as mottled gray as — squint squint — the actual — crap — actual spider webs spun throughout the trees by what had to be giant ass spiders.

(How'd he miss those spider webs?!)

He smelled their musty spidery smell from here yet he

hadn't noticed them. Idiot. Better not let Sieg and his asspad know.

The three cat girl figures blended in so well— squint squint — two grey-blue the other orange and black — the green figure hadn't noticed them yet.

The green figure was Leena, their lustdream-come-true companion.

The other green figures were more mottled green and in groups. They had to be the orcs. A few of the mottled green figures stayed low in the spider web trees and had bows and with arrow ready.

Orc archers. Most were near the ground.

The dimming of the light was another bad sign. The cherry sunset was progressing fast (like usual this time of year) and his stomach grumbled for the meal that wouldn't come for hours now.

Even a taste of piss-quality ale sounded good right about now.

The perfect reason to survive this mess.

So his other hand was already on the pommel of his saber dagger. One of two saber daggers. Relieved the blades only looked like blue steel but was actually cold silver, one of the best anti-dark metals in existence.

"Look there," Roo said, "Three tigresses. The bitches are teaming up on ... Leena."

"You only realized that now," Sieg said, "Interesting. Sad too."

"We need to help her," Roo said and slipped his hand over to his revolver crossbow.

The hand-sized gun could fire up to seven small arrows per cylinder and he had several pre-loaded cylinders in his pouch. The arrow's blades were demon-loathed cold silver and thus extra pricey, but being a Knight paid well, and it paid to spent extra money into staying alive.

To top it off, he even had the string of the bow forged from cat gut, as in lycan girl tigress gut, from an extra tough tigress hedgie he personally took out.

The bone bow was forged from a sturdy yet flexible blend of bone from a tigress master of their magical martial arts and the shell of a spidora swordmaster.

Both from tough darklings he personally took out.

"You can't hit them from here," Sieg said.

Finally.

The High Prince speakth.

But Roo hated when Sieg was right.

And right now, Sieg was just too right.

"I know," Roo said, "But ..."

"But nothing," Sieg said, "Don't interfere."

Figures.

But his authority over fellow knights ... far more limited.

Roo's beloved revolver crossbow could only hit a target within a few dozen yards at best. The added distance from the thousand foot cliff wouldn't add enough distance to reach any of the three tigresses planning on ambushing Leena.

The noise of the arrow landing so far away, worthless except for warning tigress of more trouble was coming.

Yelling here wouldn't help Leena. Even if her pointy

dagger elf ears could hear him, the tigresses would too, and ambush her before she could react.

But do nothing ... hell no.

"Knights help everyone in need," Roo said, "Especially other knights. Didn't you pay attention in class?"

Roo whispered. "Razz ..."

"As I recall," Sieg said, "You copied from my notes more often than not, but judging from your exam grades, your memory isn't the best so you misremembering the truth, not surprising. I'm more surprised you remembered that odd stray comment Crow said only once at the beginning of the first class. How you manage do remember that and barely anything else ..."

"Aye aye Cap'," Razz said, "But Leena promised me better corpses than herself too and elf girl corpses, the best."

"Well darklings corpses shall rain from the sky soon enough," Sieg said, "Demon Ender will soon be ready. My asspad is warming up nicely and ..."

Popping up over Roo, Razz suddenly enlarged himself to Roo's own size. Swooped down. Snatched Roo by the shoulders. Easily lifting him.

While swooping down the cliff.

Down the valley toward Leena.

Down very very quickly but detail details.

Knowing full well Sieg would refuse to curse out loud, let alone yell at from at this point, but swear he would.

All the more perfect.

FOUR

Leena knew something was off about this forest.

The smell ... no forest should remind her of the dark echoing depths of the abandoned well among the rubble of that long lost ancient human town near her home.

Before demons destroyed it.

This place sent a tingle down her spine no mountain blizzard ever matched.

Even when ... braving a mountain blizzard nude was among the last and worse tests an elf warrior in training must conquer.

The chill in the still air was nothing to a blizzard's chill.

The endless spiderwebs were those of giant black widowers. The demonic kind. Demons of the dark, phantoms of no substance until they fused with actual spiders that were all too common in her former homeland. They mutated into the giant spiked horrors that prowled here hidden in the darkest shadows.

Such spiders didn't need regular prey to sustain themselves. Just souls. Of beasts and men.

And elves.

The upper section of the forest had grown twisted and thick, just like the spiderwebs. The influence of the demons and their physical form.

The batches of leaves were even stranger. They left the taste of bitter rotting blueberry in her mouth and that's only when she got a couple paces too close.

Some kind of toxin?

No. Another kind of demon? Another physical form?

Maybe.

It reminded of bittersweet memories of home. Memories best not thought of now.

But the slimy feel of the air grew worse and worse whenever she got too close to the ground.

The ground looked like the normal dark soil of a healthy forest, yet ... there wasn't a single leaf down there.

Not even a stray twig. or broken branch.

It was too clean for a forest.

Even the most well-tended ones had more clutter than this forest.

Leena knew better than to dig too deep here. Their goal was to get inside the pyramid, or, at least, gather the right information on it then use a telejournal, a journal linked to one other journal, and to let their superior Crow know the critical details. Whether it really did spell the end of mankind if the ritual was started — a ritual called the Epochal Play.

A silly name for such a serious matter. She was relieved her companion Roo didn't know of it yet.

Or even Sieg.

Their lustdream-come-true quips were annoying but expected. At least she knew they wouldn't try to munch her for a meal after trying to bed her, like a few of nastier lust-dream-come-true demons that had chased after her.

Worse, bedded elf women were too weak to defend themselves for too long after the bedding, so of course, all kinds of monsters would try to bed or rape elf women, but none of those knights needed to know that.

Ever.

Assuming they didn't already.

She ran along these thick branches. Avoiding the demonic spiders was easily enough for one of her skill. The orcs gave their position away from their horrible cries.

They were far too close.

But on the ground. Thank the Oak of Lightful Ages.

As rough as it was, she had to admit the dragon scale clothing of knights was more protective than any sungwood armor common among her kind. Even the greenest wood with the most circles of life sung to a bright sunny yellow.

Like her twin daggers.

The white tricross of a sword in winged stone, the emblem for not just a True TriCross Knight, but a Templar of the Light. She didn't mind the emblem woven into her dragon scale.

They all had such emblems.

But cold silver was mildly toxic to some elves. Elves with lycan blood raped into them. Her bastard of a father ...

Her mother escaped, thank the Oak of Lightful Ages, and her kind raised Leena as an elf, not as a lycan monster.

But Leena never showed off her furry form.

Not around other elves.

Or even lightlings. Ever.

But that toxicity was nothing compared to how cold silver affected demons. It was toxic enough that Leena didn't want her companions questioning her fidelity to the Light, so she did her best to avoid cold silver as best she could.

Although she suspected if she let Roo touch her chest, especially her bare chest in elven form, even just once, he'd stop questioning anything about her very quickly, hoping too much for much more.

Why she was thinking of Roo rather than the studly Sieg ... sigh. She knew Sieg would bed and forget her, as much as her heart trembled around him and hoped for more, that handsome guy, his smell, a smell of a strong man that could destroyed any demon that dared try to violate her.

Unlike Roo. A goofball.

Useless and annoying most of the time.

But decent intentions ... most of the time. he might not slay her if he found out about her other form. Her lycan blood, but Sieg certainly would.

That talking crow of Roo's should of delivered the news by now. But maybe not. Her information might be too techni-cal. Even talking crows couldn't carry some news well — like the technical details of a building's structure — as much as they aspired to.

As the legends often claimed.

Deep down, Leena was sure there was more than just the Epochal Play to worry about here.

If her suspicions were correct.

She needed to take this detour on the way back. Neither of her companions could climb up or down that cliff that was the closest thing to an entry way into this valley.

The Valley of Deathly Shadow.

Sieg might pretend to listen ... Roo ... no. Least Roo was direct about his idiocy.

Most of the time.

In the air, that extra chill, something even worse was coming. Worse than orcs or lycan.

Good thing none of her companion were here.

They'd just get in the way.

But she mustn't reveal her awareness.

Yet.

Countering the coming ambush — critical to surviving this.

And maybe the key to unlock this mess.

CHAPTER

FIVE

Roo was well above the valley. Razz carrying him.

But the air tasted far too musty for this wide open space. The air should smell clean and fresh. Not musty.

Or so cold. The wind wasn't *that* strong.

The many hints of slimy disgusting orc weren't unexpected. They loathed baths as much as they loathed any hint of the Light. No scent of lycan furball either, but that kind of stake fodder wasn't that dumb. They were a higher class of fodder than orcs, after all. Regeneration among their females wasn't their only advantage.

They had brains and used them.

(Usually.)

((Just look at his own mother. Scholarly to the max and a gorgeous tigress to boot, even if she stayed in her human form pretty much all the time, and refused to teach Roo how to go wicked wolf boy.))

(((But one day he'd figure it out.)))

Leena wouldn't escape by herself easily.

Razz got them lower and lower and ...

The oaks really were shaped cobwebs of thick wood plus plenty of real genuine spiderwebbing from giant black spiders lingering in the shadows yet something was off ...

Mental check and good — his belt still had a baker's dozen of steel stakes strapped snug. They were for that close up distance strike when pounding them dead would take too long.

Many tigresses often had throwing daggers, and unlike lightling dagger throwers who could only throw accurately at a specific distance, tigresses were unique among demons of the dark because they could throw daggers accurately and quickly for a range of distances.

Kinda like their pouncing abilities.

These feline lycan were all blue-grey with white belly and chest fur, yet they blended in too well with the murky woods below.

Everything seemed to slow down, drastically, as they got closer and closer and closer, winding tasting mustier and mustier and ick — more feline — down to the last few dozen yards to the ~~crashing~~ landing point.

As every instructor for every knight ever taught Roo, observe the enemy before striking ...

(If you can.)

(See? Roo did listen. Sometimes. His old man, but first and his second father both taught him far more anyway.)

(And sleeping through his mother's lectures was a good way to earn a clawing.)

(And how she managed to claw him without anyone else noticing what she was … rumor had it she and his old man fought for weeks on end before … well … his first brother was conceived and enemies went to lovers and ugh.)

(But his old man did teach him how to safely remove those awful slaving collars.)

So in that first slooooow moment, Roo ignored Razz the Giant Real Crow squeezing his shoulders even tighter.

Mother's sly clawings build more than enough endurance for random, if not deserved, pain.

Instead Roo carefully noted the closest cat girl to Leena.

A blue-grey tigress. About a dozen feet behind Leena.

Several sprints up higher along the same twisting, thick branch as Leena.

If there's multiple enemies, nickname them quick for simpler thinking, as Crow often said, and that birdman Crow was technically their superior now, not just their instructor.

So Roo dubbed that cat girl Boob Eyes.

Because Boob Eyes had fat stripes almost like spots of a leopard except stretched, especially two choice stripes on her big boobs that make them look like bulging eyeballs. Her long locks of golden hair gave those boob eyes eyebrows and gave her chest a snarling expression.

More snarling than her actual facial expression.

Her black shoulder belt was full of wicked black dagger.

Cold iron daggers. The throwable kind. Her black belt held a pair of crimson iron claw extenders around her slim waist.

Typical weaponry of tigresses.

But otherwise bare in the fur. Fur was good enough for those furballs.

(And ... only few yards closer. Really? How did Razz fly so slowly and stay in the air? It wasn't magic. Razz was a hedgie crow and his other magical trick — I mean, Hedge, (and yes capital H because Hedges were formally *Very* **Important**), but his Hedge wasn't superslow flight.)

So plenty of time till crash time.

Plenty of time to observe the next tigress.

Close behind Boob Eyes. Yet quite a bit higher.

The branch she was running down was pretty damn steep. Her razor claws kept her steady. Below their knees their legs were like the hind quarters of a tiger anyway. Allowed them to pounce and gut with powerful kicks.

So Roo dubbed that next tigress the Platinum Ditz.

Because she was adorably striped light blue over lighter grey. It blended perfectly well with her pure white and fluffy belly and chest fur. And those doeishly big pale blue eyes proclaimed a (very fake) terrified innocence in her low nervous gait.

A gait full of wallflowered ditziness Roo spotted in plenty of human village girls. Especially after they noticed his dragon scale outfit and its emblem.

But that was genuine wallflowered ditziness in human girls.

Even odder, the Platinum Ditz had crazy ass-long hair ...

so crazy ass long it looked like a long very neat mop of the finest pale sunny hair that ... hmmm.

(Thinking about it, Roo could really use good mop for the All Summer Eve festival clean up ... and Razz squeezing his shoulders to the breaking just then ... okay okay, moving on ... sigh, ouch ouch, okay. Razz knew Roo all too well.)

Anyway, just like Boob Eyes, the Platinum Ditz had a shoulder belt and a waist belt. But ... her claw weapons were blue steel, not crimson steel? Strange. Lycan were especially weak to cold silver, so it couldn't be cold silver. It exhausted their regeneration quick. Enough to exhaust them to beautiful valuable corpses.

And her belts were pale blue leather. Not a single hint of cobweb on them.

Somehow.

(Interesting. When he looked at those belts, a tingle kept zipping a chill down his spine.)

(Maybe they were stray relics that got mixed in with genuine clothing and relics were crazy rare, but they let anyone use a spell as powerful as a wizard or witch and without a serious limitation like real magic either. Even if they weren't relics, those belts would go from some good coin — ouch ouch ouch — okay Razz.)

(Really moving on this time.)

The third one, on a branch crisscrossing the one Leena was on. This one was right above the Platinum Ditz and partly hidden by another toupee of oak leaves. Right above the Platinum Ditz was the orange tigress Roo dubbed Sexy Stripes. Mainly because crisscrossing her black stripes were so sultry suggestive that you'd think she was bred for perverts.

Yeah. Slavomancers were big pervs.

Including that fact she had the most amazing and gigantic aerodynamic boobage on a cat girl Roo had ever seen.

Or maybe it was the white fluff of fur between those boobs.

Toss in the most slender waist and wow, definitely elf girl in that one. Lycan captured and ate so many elf girls, killing far more many elf guys in the process, that crossbreeding rape was bound to occur. Her red shoulder and waist belts — daggers all the darkest of crimson iron.

At least the lush wedge of black hair over the side of her pixie mawed face hid Roo and Razz from her indirect sight.

And those big bright green eyes were definitely hungry for the kill.

Razz weaved through the spiderweb of branches easily.

Slow flight was sure convenient. It must of made avoiding the countless actual spiderwebs a whole lot easier.

And these actual spiderwebs were cobwebs so huge and thick they might be big enough to trap Razz while fully enlarged too.

(Finally, the last couple few dozen yards. Go Razz!)

(Stop squeezing!)

(Okay okay only another dozen yards to enter that twisting maze of crazy thick branches and toupee leave bunches and thick, thick spiderwebs.)

Now why hadn't Leena noticed him and Razz yet ... strange.

Least the tigresses hadn't either.

She still was dashing down the branch near the top of the oak ... very very veeery slowly because— oh yeah.

Adrenaline rush. That's it. Not magic. Good.

Phew.

Unknown limitations were often bad news.

Oh yeah. Better start aiming his revolver crossbow now.

At Boob Eyes, of course, the closest tigress.

And aiming ... shit.

Just moving his hand ... soooooo slow.

But all elf maidens were renowned for their badassery archery and warrioring.

Only reason there's still elves left actually.

Yet Leena not noticing three tigresses chasing her — yikes, that was outright careless. Not badass at all. Boob Eyes and the Platinum Ditz were only a dagger toss away by now.

Daggers in their hands too.

Sexy Stripes, oh boy, in a few sprints and a jump to another branch coming up, Sexy Stripes would soon to be right above Leena.

Never mind the orcs hording over the ground below. In grubby mottled green cowls and cloaks and pointy spears and axes.

Stinky and screechy orcs.

With torches that were setting the musty tree alit.

The billowing blinding dark smoke closing in.

And the tigresses waiting for it too.

CHAPTER

SIX

Like thousands of times back at home, Sieg made a point not to grind his teeth, grimace, or even shift forward, and this time it was far easier not to shift forward. Because forward was toward that thousand foot plummet, toward that wretched idiot and his overgrown crow flapping like a boulder tossed by another catapult.

No.

The sunset was a beautiful red. It was as bright and sweet as the cherry sundae he enjoyed every Saintly Sunday to remind himself of the joys of being a High Prince and the next in line to be High King.

The ice it was made from was just like the ice of the glaciers covering the peaks long before reaching this treacherous valley.

The sun was still as golden as his dragon scale suit. The clouds still as white as his emblem.

Of course, he had worked hard to earn the right to wear this outfit, more or less, just to see what it was like to work to earn something important but, in truth, he was one of the Lightest Ones, as was right and proper.

No one but a Chosen one, whether Darkest One or Lightest One, could kill him.

But cripple him — or break him — yes, that was more than possible by anyone, even rank bow fodder, but a Chosen One had luck of their side — until they were up against another Chosen. So in the end, there was no safely avoiding combat against highly experienced warriors and mages.

But strangely, that nervousness he once called fear proved also to be excitement. It proved his lessers even wronger than he knew they were.

The same nervous he had right now.

The chill in the wind, that Rowan fool hadn't noticed it until too late.

No doubt he noticed it on the way down.

The smell of must, like cobwebs in a part of a castle rarely visited by the servants, it was just a disguise, like the red fox masks at the All Hallows Eve festival.

His asspad of a sword still grumbled at losing the word-play exchange with Rowan and Razz, but no matter. This very sword was a major clue to his true identity and the key to his survival. So Sieg stood tall waiting for the inevitable encounter that was coming.

Rowan hid his own truth closer and better than he realized, as much as Sieg hated to admit it, and it was one reason Sieg also carried a barbed cold silver dagger.

Just in case.

The oaks behind him were thick, craggy, and forked like the tongues of the countless courtiers at court. The bramble left few passages between the tree, but luckily they found this ledge. It was the only location any of them could get a good view of the Temple of the Forsaken Foxling God.

Never mind foxlings were a darkling long wiped out in the last cycle's War between Light and Darkness. Vixen lycan a poor excuse of a throwback to foxlings.

Not a rebirth. Thank the Light.

The gold plating was so elaborate Sieg almost laughed.

Almost.

The reflection of what should of been the sun, a lighter gold, was in fact the pitch black of the abyss. A reminder that all foxling kind had been returned to the abyss from whence they came and suffered horribly for their failure to wipe out mankind, or even elven kind.

The pink outline of the black, Sieg couldn't explain. He'd never seen that shade of pink before. Witch girls wore ... a lighter friendlier shade of it.

The stack of grimoires the temple was modeled after were ... bizarre and disturbing in their bone and demon theme. The obsession with pearls too. No sign of anything fox, strangely enough, as if its true nature had to remain hidden.

Too much like the gothic wizard who advised his royal parents.

Why this golden temple hadn't been stripped down by thieves ... it took more than wild demons to keep determined thieves out.

A girlie giggle came from too close behind him.

Sieg made a point not to react.

Yet.

His asspad did the reacting for him.

"Ah!" said Demon End, "A darkling worthy of my Razor edge! Come quench my thirst for darkling blood!"

"Oh how polite, no?" said the girl, "But vhat can a girl expect from zee asspad."

"Silke Snow," Sieg said, "Or did you lose that name with your pelt? My humble apologies."

The angry huff. Good.

The girl Sieg knew as the gorgeous vixen witch Silke Snow. All snow vixens were named Snow by their Great Darkness to demean them and keep their arrogant nature in check. But all darklings nowadays had to earn their own given name and any failure ... possibly lose it too.

"But I am just Snow," the vixen said, "For now."

"And this time you'll die just as Snow too," Sieg said and turned around.

Studied her silently.

Perking her foxy ears up for those extra couple of inches. Like she was some idiotic baron of minor but overproud blood, Snow stood her six full feet on the tallest boulder right beyond the most bramble-shaped oak.

That she was far more shapely than Leena ...

So shapely that had she not been a darkling, Sieg would of considered bedding her, despite her being covered in beautiful white short fur, a foxy cute snout instead of a human mouth and nose and fluffy fox tail.

By her appearance, she belonged in a child's tale as another busty heroine or even a femme fatale, but no, her Great Darkness knew better than to make all its minions disgusting bloodthirsty horrors.

She clearly caught his flicker of desire and flicked her wedge of golden hair dismissively at him. She winked with those big blue eyes at him, as if adding a sneaky maybe.

Made his heart ache foolish.

"Staring is so rude, Monsieur Sieg," Silke said, "Vhy not just paint me, no?"

That lowly foreign honorific for *mister* rather than the proper honorific for Lord *Sire*, or even the more formal *Monseigneur*, and her romantically nasal accent ... it was as if this snow vixen was really from the most romantic kingdom of the known world, Fiona Shar.

She even gave that famous pouty look of girls from that city, despite her having a foxy snout rather than a human mouth and nose.

"I'll paint you red with blood," Sieg said.

"Red is so romantic, no?" Silke said, "It vould be rude, but you are clearly stunned by my beauty."

She even giggled sinister.

"A zecond chance to end you," Silke said, "The Great Darkness it truly great, no?"

Sieg hesitated for a reason. Witches could master as many Hedges as they could train themselves, and Silke's abilities were as superb as her gorgeous looks.

"And a good reason to pelt you again," Sieg said, "Before ending you. For good this time."

Her fur would hold some of her power. Now there used to be even more than Hedges, according to the wizard that advised his parents, but that knowledge was lost to the ages, yet Crow his ... superior ...

As much as Sieg hated to admit having a superior, even if it was as only as a knight, Crow would still certainly find uses for a vixen witch's corpse.

Worse, Silke looked completely fresh. Full of stamina.

"Zhen come get me," Silke said, "My fur is as beautiful as me — he-he."

She posed energetic and sultry like an eager courtesan. Her fur trim and not a single fur strand off. Despite this being the middle of nowhere. With her razor claws she combed her wedge of golden hair to the left lush and neat, as if she was combing herself all the way here, as if she were some sensible human.

There wasn't even the slightest sign of exhaustion.

And one limitation lycan witches had, and it was more extreme than hedgies — the more magic they used the less regeneration they could do before exhaustion killed them.

It helped that every slice Demon Ender sucked in several times the lycan stamina otherwise needed to heal and quickly drained their ability to regeneration and stay alive.

Rumor had it lycan witches could even exhaust themselves to death using magic, but Sieg wasn't sure of it.

Yet.

Too few lycan witches to try the idea out on.

Time to end their silent mutual glaring.

"I shall," Sieg said, "Bare in the beautiful fur this time too.

Not even a belt or two for claw extenders or daggers. Your Darkness must be quite upset at you."

Silke pouted. "I have no need for such trivialities, no? My magic ..."

Sieg drew Demon Ender. "Won't save you."

But with a shrug, she created her own claw extensions of razor blue ice.

Then blue ice bikini armor too, arrogantly enough to match the skimpy and ridiculously suggestive styles of Fiona Shar too, in actual battle, as if she didn't know her magic would only feed his blade.

"Ah, yes, nearly forgot," Silke said, "Zee asspad can cut through my magic, but like a gluttonous troll ..."

That sly look of hers ... caution was needed. He knew from their last fight she didn't use Hedges that used conversational triggers as traps. It was a limitation imposed by her rather powerful offensive magic.

She slashed at him. Not moving from her spot.

Menacing arcs of blue light shot right at him.

He sliced back.

CRACK!

CRACK!

They struck his blade. The impact.

Like they were powerful blade strikes themselves.

Forced him back.

Sieg made a point not to grimace.

Silke giggled. "I call zhem my Sight Slicers. Guess why."

She slashed more at him.

So many Sight Slicers he could barely see her.

One by one. Quick.

He deflected them all.

But each forced him back more.

And more.

Such a powerful impact ...

Sieg sighed. "Pathetically uncreative."

"Really?" Silke said, "Zhen ..."

Silke slashed another flurry of Sight Slicers.

The cracks. The smell of broken stone?

Their ends ripped right through boulder!

(No dragon scale would save him from them.)

Sieg blocked.

Blocked.

Blocked.

An endless barrage of Sight Slicers.

But Sieg. would. not. relent.

Each Sight Slicer. must take more. effort on her part. than him. blocking.

Then ... ah!

A double Sight Slicer! Criss-crossed!

Sieg heaved his Demon Ender at it—

CLANK!

And he flew back. Feet catching. Sliding on mossy rock.

Flying.

Onto another rock. Sword into stone.

Screeching.

Crashing into another rock.

Thumping onto ground.

And to a halt.

Silke sighed. "Almost. My Twin Sight Slicer has quite zee bang to it, no?"

"Almost?" Sieg said, "Almost only counts in horseshoes and boom darts."

Boom.

The whole ledge shuttered.

"I mean," Silke said, "Almost *ready*."

SEVEN

After Roo blinked, choked through the puff of smoke.

A puff of smoke more obnoxious than gramps and his endless lectures over the awful of cat girls and Roo's own lycubi mother blah blah blah.

After another moment of fighting back the tears from the smoke biting his bare eyeballs worse than some dramatic sob story of a play.

Tears that would only signal weakness.

Better red eyes than tearing.

And a final moment of spitting out the tarrish taste nipping his mouth worse than some dirty teething pup back when he did somehow go wolf boy for a day and ended up muddier than a mud slime.

Roo finally noted something actually worse.

Something Crow would of shook his head in disappointment for neither Roo or Leena noticing earlier.

Leena's own branch — it was running out.

And it was only clear to Roo now.

From his vantage point.

The branch ended at the next twist around a crazy thick trunk, and the trunk was full of slimy slick moss, so no going ant girl and running up or down it to safety.

It was an actual dead end.

Double shit.

The bad part was that the curve ensured Leena wouldn't notice until it was too late. The only branches close by were covered in so much moss that if she played grasshopper elf there was no hope she'd land without slipping off.

The dragon scale on the soles of her boots would only provide so much gripe. He knew how much. He had the same on his. Just a different color.

And right now Razz would need a cool down of ten minutes or so before he could enlarge again. Even then, he wasn't strong enough to lift both Roo and Leena out of here.

Or slow a fall to the ground. Not when it was so far far far down below.

And yet ...

Ack.

Speeding up again? And ... half another dozen paces closer.

(Of course, adrenaline nonsense. Rushes were deadly due to misjudging the slow down effect.)

Okay. Slowly speeding up.

Crap.

From magical backlash making the adrenaline rush craziness crazier. It wasn't a limitation he imposed on himself for his own Hedge. Nor did Razz impose it.

Maybe Leena?

Normally the adrenaline rush should speed up quick and suddenly.

Not so slowly.

So the last couple dozen yards before the first crash point ... passing by. A few more veers.

Good.

Razz aimed to get in closer. With so many branches and spiderwebs twisting and cobwebbing around the place, Razz veered and swooped and veered and swooped and wow.

Amazing.

Even more amazing, Roo managed (finally) to aim at Boob Eye's heart.

Normally staking a lycan would only paralyze the bitch completely — not kill it or even start exhausting it to death. Unless staked with cold silver or another anti-dark material. The material would then also drain its regeneration and (eventually) exhaust it to death.

(Rumor had it they used to be easier to kill but something happened kinda recently ...)

Speeding up more. Talky time.

Just don't talk with the tigresses or else, if they were hedgies, they might — no, they usually used chit chat to trigger one of their more dangerous Hedges.

Seduce and slash style.

Okay, the chit chat was technically a limitation, but it doubled as a booby trap, and these bitches all have enough serious big boobage to make a guy really really stupid no matter the fur covering them.

(Another reason cat girls like them were nicknamed lycubi.)

And now, only a couple dozen yards and a few more branches between them and the feline targets. Speeding up more.

Veering around last branch in … 1.

"Those tigresses look too shapely for …" Roo said, "Lycan shift into human forms, not elf girls, but they have that sexy elf girl physique like Leena, and that's despite all that short fur and kitty crap."

"Tasty elf girl quality lycan," Razz said, "Puuuurrrrfect."

Boob Eyes looked up at Razz. Finally.

Talk objective achieved.

She winked.

(Why? Because she's an evil cat. That's why.)

She even grinned wicked.

(Creepy.)

"It's rrrraining mice," Boob Eyes said, "How sweet of you."

Uh huh.

Click. Roo shot her in that big blue eye.

Full speed.

She howled. Stumbled back. Off the branch.

And thumped on the soggy ground. Thrashed yowling.

Leena spun around. Finally.

"I hate cats!" Leena said.

The Platinum Ditz stumbled. Stuttered. Dagger in hand.

Threw it.

"A-a-a-and we h-h-h-hate — ack!" the Platinum Ditz said.

Leena shot the Platinum Ditz in the heart.

While she dodged the dagger Ditz flung her way.

But another dagger came at her. From Sexy Stripes.

At Leena's face.

Roo flung a steel stake at it. Hard.

CLANK!

Cold iron dagger deflected by steel stake. Good. Saved Leena's face. Slow down almost gone.

"I saw that," Leena said, "But nice save."

And she shot at Sexy Stripes.

Hit the branch underneath the tigress.

"Nice miss," Roo said, "You thin off their orc loves. I'll—"

Sexy Stripes spat. "Hurt my lovelies? Those wonderfully disgusting — HISSS!"

An arrow zipped through Sexy Stripes' big pointy kitty ear.

Her flesh regenerated almost as quick as it left her.

"Slimy as an orc," Leena said, "No wonder I keep missing this fleabag."

"My fleas are adorable!" Sexy Stripes said and — oh crap.

A horde of flea leapt off her and grew bigger and bigger and bigger.

And transformed into a bunch flea-themed midget knights from right out of a little brat's goofy story.

Which meant unlike large monstrous fleas — these

bastards could actually fight with their bladed limbs and block with their shielded bits.

Which they did. Blocked several of Leena's arrows.

As skillfully as Sieg's annoying knight guards.

(Knight guards that they happened to have ditched a week ago.)

(Again.)

But thank the Light Razz swooped them down behind Sexy Stripes.

Sure, he reverted to normal crow size.

And dropped Roo on … *OUCH.*

On a very big, very black spider.

One with a very spiky shell that thank the Light for the protective dragon scale all knights were granted on graduation day from the Academy.

(And the cup he added for that extra protection down under.)

The spider hissed louder than the tigress.

Sure, the spider had been hidden in the giant cobweb right beside Sexy Stripes. Ready to munch her.

Leena sighed. "Saving everyone in need … even darklings. Rowan, you —"

The spider bucked Roo fiercer than the furious longhorn minotaur he tried grabbing a drinking horn from. A longhorn drinking horn … a guy's dream come true.

This spider was nothing.

Roo even yanked out a cold silver dagger.

"Yeee-haw!" Roo said.

And drove the blade deep into the spider's head.

Just as Sexy Stripe's flea knights slashed at Leena.

Leena dodged.

"I am used to cat fights," she said, "Not flea fights."

The fleas were as dark brown as the trees and easily blended in. Not made of cold iron, thank the Light. So a few scratches wouldn't be deadly to her.

Unlike cold iron.

One scratch from cold iron and one dead elf girl.

CHAPTER

EIGHT

These fleas and their lycan master ...

Not the ambush Leena intended to counter but as the Oak of Lightful Ages grows the strangest branches ...

The branch she was backing up on, retreating on was still thick enough for her to dodge sideways, but only for a step or two. At most.

Then the slant of the bark got too treacherous.

her back was approaching the trunk of the tree, but the smell of the moss on it — too much of the abandoned well of her childhood home.

Strange.

No spiderwebs were close by.

Unfortunately, Rowan had inadvertently saved her tigress opponent from the spider, but the spider web left behind might still be useful. Leena knew the spider Rowan leapt onto was not a nestling, thus, no more spiders to ...

Wait.

The crackling behind that orange tigress.

The web was shaking too.

At that moment Leena was glad for the dragon scale on the bottom of her boots. For the protective dragon scale over herself.

The fleas were too much like multilimbed gnome knights with mandible-clicking helms. Shields and blades apart of their natural armor.

Even a regular bow and arrow would not do.

Against actual knights the joints were the weak points. Those points would, at beast, only be protected by chain, but an elven bow and arrow could punch through most steel.

Unless it was spelled or dwarf forged.

But her true elven bow and arrows of amber light, which could punch through even dwarf forged armor, no, it would draw the wrong attention if she used them again so soon.

She could sense the thing she needed to be on guard against stirring ... and ...

The fleas hesitated. No. Preparing.

They were still growing larger. The size ... not gnomes, not half her height, but two thirds of it.

Of dwarves!

Their tigress mistress hid behind the branch above Leena. Not a hint of her orange fur or black stripes were visible. Too protected now to attack directly unless—

The fleas all attacked.

At once.

Leena shot the joints of the closest.

All deflected.

But the punch of her shots threw them off. Made them collide against each other.

Slowed them down further.

Leena backed up quick.

They all landed. Scrambled apart. Clicked a strange language.

The closest charged.

The rest leapt.

All with good space between them. Her arrows useless.

The fleas would soon land behind her. Beside her. On her. And the chargers blocked her way forward.

She tossed her bow.

Drew her daggers.

And sang.

Her Hedge — Moss Shield.

It could deflect up to fourteen strikes at most before breaking for a sunful hour, unless she let it recover before it broke by not using any Hedge for a second per deflected hit.

Of course, like anything worn when she activated this Hedge, her dragon scale armor transformed into her cringe-worthy skin-suit of far too revealing moss. It set her heart aflutter for all the wrong reasons. Made it hard to concentrate.

Not jolt awkward and stupid.

No matter what part of her body, covered or ... not, it would deflect the strikes.

Even the otherwise deadly stabs to her nearly bare chest.

And she could move best using the power of the strikes deflected. This embarrassingly revealing nature of this moss skin-suit, this embarrassing weakness allowed her to magnify the power of the deflected strikes — with all the power of these insanely heavy flea knights behind the strikes — and reflect an even more intense counter.

To her stomach.

Legs.

The fleas who struck now exploded.

Several attacks to her back.

Several more fleas exploded.

The chargers reached her. Attacked.

Exploded.

Two more strikes left before her shield broke.

The tigress shrieked. Right above Leena now.

"My fleas!" the tigress said, "Avenge your comrades!"

More flea knights landed around Leena. Their legs stabbed the wood deep. As if readying for something worse than a charge or leap.

Three in back. Three in front.

And two over her — boom. boom.

CRACK

Moss shattered into the air. Dusting her insides like sawdust as she gasped. Her dragon scale outfit returned tight and snug and protective.

But not protective enough.

Moss Shield was gone for a full fourteen seconds — unless no!

Not yet.

She activated the Moss Shield Hedge again — but a useless version of it. Survive this battle and she'd gain use of it again.

And maybe evolve it. Get more strikes.

For now only one Hedge left.

The one Hedge most elves had. Were famous for.

And counters well known.

CHAPTER

NINE

Roo grimaced.

Held on tight to his cold silver dagger. Like a saddle stick thingie when riding a horse. Except this was a spider. A very big, very black, and very nasty spider. And the stick thingie was the hilt of a cold silver blade driven into its head.

Sadly no saddle.

So thank God he did have dragon scale on.

And a cup on underneath.

(Thank the Light.)

No telling how many more spiders were lurking in the countless cobwebs gluing the endless toupees of leaves together.

No doubt the only thing they usually got to munch were squirrels because squirrels were probably one of the only little critters stupid enough to try living in a forest full of giant hungry spiders.

Of course, Roo hadn't see any squirrels yet. Not even their little itty bitty bones so maybe not. Those little furballs weren't smart enough to avoid all these webs.

But what did these spiders eat when nothing else was around. Too many of these webs were empty. Too many hungry spiders led to a bunch of dead spiders.

No spider corpses on these twisting wooden spiderwebs trees either.

No matter.

He vised his spider with his legs. Shoved its head down.

Held onto his gun for dear life.

The spider charged. Around and around the twisting branch.

Through thick cobwebs.

Gave Roo a few glances at Boob Eyes on the ground.

One of her hands already learned painfully of the cold silver dust he glued onto the razor sharp feathers on all his arrows. The other hand was learning how slick the shaft was, because it was made from ground spidora shell.

It paid not to be cheap about his gun's ammo.

Roo tried to drive the spider at Boob Eyes. Let it finish the job it intended to start. Okay, start the job Roo interrupted.

But the spider resisted.

Resisted very very well. It leapt to a nearby branch. Twisted around and around the other branch.

Onto another trunk.

Around and around. His legs ached and ached.

Groin ... (not going there.)

But he held on for dear life.

Those spider mandibles yearned for Roo-flesh, and his dragon scale wouldn't save him from a face mauling or that dripping venom. That venom was melting moss and wood in ways nothing of this world should manage.

Another few glances at Boob Eyes, and she was down below on the lowest branch in the area.

It turned out slick spidora shaft was no match for tigress claw and wow, were those claws sharp and trim to get a grip on it.

(Then again, his mother did warn him never to underestimate a tigress' claws ...)

The Platinum Ditz was flat on her back only a few paces below Boob Eyes. Those pitiful wide-eyes ... just paralyzed. Not dead.

Not yet.

Roo tried to steer the spider close to Boob Eyes but it leapt to another trunk. Moss was no deterrent to this spider and its stabby legs. It even slid away from the felines at an angle.

But toward the ground.

Right over the orcs below.

Orc arrows zipped passed. Yikes. Dragon scale good protection.

For now.

Too bad you had to leave some vulnerable space when using dragon scale or else. Since coverage beyond a certain max, there'd be unnaturally high odds of being hit in a vulnerable spot, and the more covered passed that max the higher those unnatural odds would go.

Roo tried to aim another shot at Boob Eyes.

Yank.

Jolt.

Nope. The spider was too furious and shaky.

Boob Eyes finally ripped the arrow out of her eye. Eye quickly regenerated.

Her fur wasn't muddy somehow, but it looked more haggard than before.

Good.

She was nearing her limit already. Hit her limit and she'd drop dead of exhaustion ... sooner or later.

Roo tried. Failed to veer the spider in the right direction.

It bucked.

And bucked.

Then slipped off the branch.

CHAPTER

TEN

Boom.

The ground shook under Sieg.

Cracked. Smelled of broken stone. Like the chalk his tutor was far too fond of.

But no gunpowder. So not a boom dart?

He stood tall, as steady as he could, but every inch of his six feet of solid brawn shook like the gelatin deserts his parents loved too much.

Rumbled now.

Rumbled worse than Rowan's stomach at a keg-full tavern. After a long hard and dry mission.

Boom. boom. boom.

From the forest behind Silke?

The trees were shaking. Branches breaking. Smashing into bramble. Breaking it.

Sieg slid backwards. The ledge must be weakening. Only paces behind him was a thousand foot fall.

His suede boots and dragon scale soles not enough.

The slippery moss was worse than any slippery courtier at court. Even the slim and "studly" creep Count Dekuth. The boulders around Sieg should keep him from sliding off the cliff, just like his position's responsibilities helped him evade long drawn out conversations with Count Dekuth.

Hopefully.

Ah. The smell of the woods and its musk hit him like a troll's club. Of wet rotting wood. Of trampled soil recently overturned. Nothing one of his sycophants could understand or tolerate.

Did Silke summon undead plants?

Boom.

He slipped back even more. The lumpy ground wasn't slowing him down his slide enough.

How much more room did he have? Falling from the cliff would certainly break him. Even if he wouldn't die outright ... he'd be as good as dead.

The dragon scale at the bottom of his suede boots wasn't enough. He needed to get to the top of the boulders, the ones not covered in so much slippery moss.

(He'd made a point of getting better scales for his soles once he got back. A High Prince had resources that his lessers did not.)

Worse the setting sun would ensure he'd lose the light soon enough. That vixen could hunt in the dark even better than her tigress sisters.

Silke even had magicked blue ice claws on her paw feet. They clearly helped her stay locked in place. That below the knees her legs were like the hindquarters of a fox meant she would try to pounce him dead like last time.

If he gave her the opening.

Which he would not. Not unless he planned to.

But Silke had all the advantages right now. Except for a weapon. Nothing she could wield could counter Demon Ender.

Booooom.

Sieg slipped. Slid back.

"Prepare yourself," said Demon Ender.

A huge shadow over him?

A glance up.

Holy ... Sieg leapt out of the way.

Slipped too much.

BOOOOOOOOOOOM.

The furry impact flung him.

Flying.

Tumbling.

Sliding to the ground.

And **crunch.** Right into a boulder.

Ouch.

Bruised bones. His dragon scale prevented worse. He twitched his whole body to double check if he could move everything. He could. Good. Nothing broken.

He stumbled back to his feet.

"A valiant try," said Demon Ender, "But useless against one such as myself."

Yes ... useless. Demon Ender could be as ridiculous as those courtier's flattering nonsense.

But Sieg choose instead to silently thank the Light for the boulder that saved him from sliding off the cliff. Luck of being a Chosen One, of course. He didn't have an overgrown crow that would save him if he fell off.

Time to start looking for a reliable flying pet.

Now Silk wasn't alone.

A big brutish troll had landed where Sieg had been.

This troll looked ... like a giant deformed vixen. Ugly and smelly as the ass of a goat with diarrhea, as Rowan might put it, and that firsthand experience ... unworthy of one such as himself, but the brown was clearly once white and ...

Another shadow over him.

He lunged more carefully this time.

BOOOOOOOOOOM! The impact!

Ack!

It flung him high.

Over the cliff.

CHAPTER

ELEVEN

R oo and his spider mount were halfway to the ground when the orcs hordes realized what happened. Cheered their blood-chilling cheers.

A few more orc arrows zipped passed too.

And a puff of smoke blocked his vision for an instant.

Like a blackout.

A nightmare of stinking burning tar. Too much like that nightmare of a night way back when but no.

Focus on the now.

But ... so much like his last memory of home. So long ago. A memory that was so distance, so tip of the tongue more, but he had rushed off to become a knight.

His heart raced now like it did back then.

Dark memories still lingered in the back of his mind. Darker than these murky spiderwebbed oaks. Cloudier than this cloud of smoke. More terrifying than getting engulfed by giant spiderwebs. More painful than this spiky spider shell against his crotch.

A sense of humor the best defense. Like his dragon scale clothing was to this spiky spider shell.

Not risking a chat about it to anyone.

Even Razz.

Deep down, he sensed shutting up was best for some reason, and with his current dumbass chatting style, no one would ever suspect he was hiding anything serious, let alone anything important.

Not even Razz.

(Roo still thanked the light his mother survived all because she was a scholar off doing scholarly stuff elsewhere.)

A gust of musty chilly air ended the tarrish nightmare. That shock of not being sure whether he was right side up or pancake side ...

Thump.

OUCH.

The spider had smacked into the ground. Roo into the spider.

Thankfully not the other way around or else squish would of went Roo.

Still, Roo squeaked silently.

His groin was NOT happy.

Thank God his cup took the worse of it. His thighs, not much happier. Only dragon scale for them.

Good enough.

For now.

The spider was dazed. Confused. Twitching from shock. But not rampaging.

Not yet.

Glancing up, those branches, wowsters, it was really high up there. Roo was surprised he hadn't broken any bones. Dragon scale was pretty amazing. No wonder dragons were so utterly hard to kill.

Leena had killed a few flea knights by … wowzers, since when did Leena dress in such slinky moss anything?

She was groin-achingly gorgeous before. Now she was even cuter, *and* cherry-tinted embarrassed. No wonder. She was by practically nude. Power-enhancing weakness right there and boy, was Roo glad for it.

A few flea knights attacked from above and boomed — wow.

Damn it.

Her dragon scale was back. At least it was form-fitting. Veeeery form-fitting. What lengths he would go to fuck her brains out … okay.

Focus.

Ah! Her scantily clad moss getup was back.

Crack.

Crack.

Those flea bastards had already broken one of two of her sungwood daggers. Paid a steep price in numbers too.

Less than a handful left. Good.

But her dark brown sungwood had weak anti-dark properties and no anti-magical properties. Why she refused cold silver …

It couldn't be from having some darkling blood in her. He had some and he had no problems with either side's beloved metal of choice, so …

Ah crap.

Ogling Leena had given Boob Eyes the chance she needed to wobble over to the Platinum Ditz, who was on the branch closest to the ground. Crap.

(Okay, worth the chance to ogle Leena nearly naked but still …)

Against these tigresses …. hmmm.

They'd no doubt have a teleport jump technique called telejump for one of their two Hedges … less limited from them too because it's a natural technique for female lycan … and most female lycan were hedgies — unlike most humans.

Even his mother had it.

Even more so than elves and their usual bow and arrows of light that they could summon on command. (Easier than carrying a big ass longbow around everywhere too. Never mind the quiver and countless arrows rattling louder than a rattlesnake.)

Boob Eyes had reached Platinum Ditz, who was still flat on the ground, paralyzed.

"See?" Boob Eyes said, "Don't hesitate, Silvia."

Crap. Lycan weren't given individual names until they earned them. They got names generic to their breed. More like their fur coats actually.

Even Roo's mother had been nameless.

That his old man dared name her Beautiful and the name stuck … so everyone else called her Bea for short …

"Here's your chance to prove you're a real Lustheart," Boob Eyes said, "You're Silvia Lustheart. I'm not about to lose my name. I just earned it too."

The Platinum Ditz was named Silvia Lustheart? Cute.

In a demented way.

He had heard here and there that lycan got real proud of earning their own names. Usually. Otherwise they had standard, easily forgettable, and very repetitive furball names since they were disposable stake fodder, after all, why bother naming them anything too distinctive?

The Platinum Ditz stumbled to her feet. "Re-Re-Re-Reena Gloryclaw, I-I-I-I'll kill h-h-him good. F-F-F-For you."

From her pale blue belt, the Platinum Ditz fumbled on her blue steel claws. Why blue steel and not the blackest of cold iron ... strange.

Her pale blue belts tingled his spine colder. Colder and closer.

Definitely relics of some sort. Relics allowed the use of a specific Hedge without the most of the limitations and restrictions a normal Hedge imposed.

Instead, if what he was taught was right, the relic would be damn taxing to use and could kill her by overuse.

Worse, the Platinum Ditz didn't look haggard at all. Just wide terrified eyes of bright pale blue. Just great. The innocent girlie act.

Something his own mother excelled at.

In both her forms.

And this Ditz's light lovely fur was far too clean for the fall she took. It gave her a pretty look that had she not been a devoted demon of the dark, she could of been someone's adorable tigress girlfriend, as fucked up as it sounded, if Roo knew how to go wolf boy ... he'd so mess with these pretty tigresses.

Except the bloody blade of Leena's arrow ... sungwood probably ... no longer in Ditz's chest.

Snap.

Boob Eyes broke the arrow and tossed it aside. Elves were renown for reusing their arrows. Figures. Lycan weren't morons like orcs were.

Sungwood was weak compared to cold silver so no big loss anyway. Why Leena didn't go with something better ... and those fluffy green feathers on the arrow?

Unlike Roo, Leena apparently didn't booby trap her arrows at all. So removing them, easy for anyone.

Including darklings.

Worse, kitty lycan were more agile. They loved themselves some ambush and ranged attacks, but a few swift jabbing attacks with claws, not a problem, but only when they were desperate.

And these two tigresses, Boob Eyes and Platinum Ditz, were desperate enough to keep their earned names.

No doubt failing their Great Darkness meant failing to keep their names.

Sure, their male brethren were all in-your-face brutal melee attacks, and worse, they had the extensive endurance to endure the punishment melee attacks exposed them to far longer than any tigress.

But Boob Eyes slipped on her cold iron claws from her black waist belt and gawked at Roo.

"What the fuck?" Boob Eyes said, "Is he ..."

"I-i-is he a spider r-r-r-r-rider?" Platinum Ditz said.

No hiding the excitement in her voice and extra big blue eyes.

Yikes.

Ditz's tail was twitching up a storm. Those stark pale blue eyes were so intense. She even flicked her mop of platinum blond hair all flirty like.

Eek.

"Yeah, baby," he said, "Want a ride in its stomach?"

Damn.

Chit chat with a tigress and she might trap him with a Hedge. How many times had his mother tricked him that way? Plenty. There was a reason they were also nicknamed lycubi.

He just risked a stupid defeat and death.

But no, not this time.

(Phew.)

Ditz simply cringed. "I-I-I ... I'll kill you!"

"You first," Roo said.

The two tigresses up and ready to fight again. They weren't nearing deathly exhaustion either.

But exhaustion wouldn't slow them down no. It would speed them up. Make them fierce until exhaust dropped them dead.

Or he dropped dead.

The screaming orcs behind him clearly intended to ensure he was the one to drop dead.

Both tigresses slipped on their claw extenders.

Vanished.

Roo readied his revolver — a howl.

To his left.

A wolf's howl.

So loud it rumbled the ground ... yikes.

Another howl. In the distance. Okay.

Not so distance.

Sounded eerily like a hollow cheer.

Shit. Not a wolf.

A wolf pack.

To his left deep in the murk ... a giant brown wolf lycan on a giant browner spider ... a giant brown recluse spider? A massive huge spider. The tigresses were already beside the wolf and had put their claw extenders away.

And drawn knives to throw his way.

Triple shit.

Only moments before they all arrived.

CHAPTER

TWELVE

He was Grendel.

He howled with every inch of his towering brawn, bone, and claw.

Let the murk know a few chills meant nothing to him.

Let the oaks try to impose their looming will on his.

As if pretending to be massive spiderwebs would impress him.

Let alone intimidate.

The smell of human blood was far better than the stink of these soggy woods full of pathetic spider demons.

The squeaks and squeals of the carts tied to their pack mule spiders only reminded him of the pigs human prey kept for their own feasting, but these carts held a lycan's feast — three villages worth of human prey. Hands all behind their backs. A bone stake driven bloody through their hands and rib latch to ensure they couldn't wiggle their hands free.

And key to keeping the lycan and orcs stationed here well fed.

A few souls for the slavomancers too.

It was times like these he had made sure his mount came from better spiderblood lines than the worthless fodder hiding and webbing the trees.

It was a true tarantula titan.

A good dozen feet off the ground and legs thick and powerful enough to rip through that pathetic dragon scale armor those tricross cowards always wore.

It could dash faster on the ground than one of those lousy spiders above could fall to the ground.

It was the fastest, the most vicious of the pack.

And the reason Grendel rode it a bit ahead of the others.

Something terrible lurked deep in these woods. Not at the pyramid the slavomancers were doing their sorcery in, no, but somewhere in these very woods, as if guarding the pyramid from all, darkling or lightling, yet it wasn't like a guard dog who'd lunge and bark at the slightest sound.

No.

The forest was so silent it could definitely hear all the creatures in it.

Maybe lord over them.

Night or day didn't matter, but the coming night only roused the urge for better prey than those worthless spiders. The lycan and orcs needed these humans to sate that lust safely. Grendel was certain that guarding creature would use hunger as a lure at some point.

Instinct from countless battles said so.

The rest of his wolves joined his howl, since with that scent in the air, there was no denying that joy.

The other scent in the air ... of dragon scale ...

Of TriCross Knights.

Every wolf in his pack had killed his share of knights. Their mastery of their own two Hedges was key.

And the very reason the slavomancers had chosen his pack, the Blood Fangs, and gave them the glory, the loot that would come with completing this mission of guarding the forest around the pyramid.

Their greatest archrivals, the Whitest Fangs, guarded the pyramid from within only because their numbers included quite a few tigresses who mastered telejump so thoroughly they could quickly telejump throughout the pyramid.

The Whitest Fangs were so desperate they even recruited that wretched trio of vixen witches.

Disgusting exotics.

There was no need for such filth. His own Hedges had killed plenty of knights like it would kill the one up ahead.

The one who just killed a horde of pathetic orcs.

He'd leave the elf to the three dubbed the Terror Titans.

Assuming those tigresses don't manage to kill her first.

Sniff sniff ... a third knight ... the vixens would fail. Let them. Then Razor Ripper would rip him apart. A little patience would guarantee that one's victory and the Razor Ripper was far more patient than Grendel himself.

The rest of the pack would guard the caged human prey.

But all would share the flesh of the dead knights.

For they were a pack. One wolf's kills were the pack's kills.

And elf flesh ... a feast worth waiting for.

THIRTEEN

Roo needed to try something desperate.

And not his Hedge.

Not yet.

While the spider was dazed, Roo listened a moment for more wolves. No way there was just one. Wolves loved to use Hedges that involved cooperation too. Stacked upon other members of their pack. Few had one Hedge. Even fewer had no Hedge, and those hedgeless wolves rarely survived long enough to get put into a pack, supposedly.

There was no doubt more of them, but the screeching orcs ... sure, his first father could kill orcs like they were ants to be stepped on, but he used his Vorshaya abilities without hesitation.

At that time there was no reason to hide the clan blood.

From the ground the forest seemed hemmed in from all the crazy thick trunks full of moss. The stinky tar smoke notwithstanding, the mustiness might not be so out of place yet ... deep in his gut ...

Not enough spiderwebs down here either. The soggy ground was so dark.

Where were all the leaves? The ground should be covered by leaves. The toupee leaf bunches should of sprinkled the ground with dead leaves. The countless spiderwebs above could only collect so many of the falling leaves. A few should of missed and reached the ground.

His stomach grumbled.

(Now? His stomach grumbles *now?*)

So despite the clanks of flea knights versus elf maiden far above his head and the spiky spider vised by his own legs, Roo holstered his revolver crossbow.

Securely holstered it.

The ground really wasn't that soggy for what he planned to do. The place wasn't that murky. The trunks of the oaks down here were big and easy to avoid too. Not like their spiderweb of branches above with all those toupee leaf bunches.

The lack of leaves down here ... the actual spiderwebs above shouldn't have caught all the leaves.

Later.

Now the orcs. Focus on them. The wolf lycan hadn't arrived.

Yet.

As his second old man grilled into him long ago, a man had to rely on his strength, and these magical tricks — I mean Hedges ... perfect if you got stuck in a corner, or a magical ambush with no other way out, but all hedgies had superhuman strength, speed, etc. etc. etc. but with his own Vorshaya bloodline, Roo focused on building those core strengths up better and better rather than perfecting his Hedges, which, was simple and straight-forward.

And given there were Hedges that could read. minds, it was best not thought of, not too much.

His strength and so on was halfway decent by now.

At least compared to his first father.

So with both hands he grabbed the cold silver dagger stuck deep in the spider's head and jolted the spider's head to the side.

And this time the spider turned.

Slightly dazed still. But turned. Slowly. Steadily. Turned. And turned.

And turned.

Going back. And forth. Back. And forth.

Stumbling.

But turning some more.

Toward the screaming orcs. A whole horde of them a couple dozen feet away and still coming. Armed to the crooked fang with spears, axes, and eek.

Firing arrows at him already.

And missed?

From so close?

Archery took practice and patience. Neither of which orcs were known for. Their minds were as deformed as their bodies.

Roo fiddled with the dagger again. But the spider refused to budge this time.

Boob Eyes laughed. "Ha! Turning his back to us!"

Ditz laughed so forced it was painful to hear. He almost felt sorry for her.

Almost.

It had to be an act. Had to be. They were called lycubi for a reason. He saw his mother play the innocent lass plenty, in both forms.

"W-w-w-we'll kill him g-g-g-good now," the Platinum Ditz said.

And their voices were closer too.

The tigresses were already prowling in for the kill and why not? He was stupid enough to expose his back. So what if he had dragon scale cloak, cowl, and jerkin on.

They might get lucky.

More orcs fired at Roo. And one arrow ... if timed right ... speaking of right timing ...

He jolted the dagger. The spider head.

Smack. An orc arrow stuck the spider in the eye.

It hissed.

Charged the orcs.

And the orcs laughed. Shot more arrows. A giant piddly spider dared challenge their whole lot.

They even hit another spider eye.

Then it was on them.

And no, their mottled green cloaks were just plain worn fabric stolen from murdered travelers. The blood and rips on the cloaks clear close up.

Until it was covered by vilely purple orc blood.

And spider rips.

The orcs died quick and horribly as they deserved. The spider took the brunt of their bladed terror and horror.

Spider shell — not as protective as dragon scale.

Soon one dying spider.

Lots of dead orcs.

And a very achy knight. One thankful he had gloves on.

CHAPTER

FOURTEEN

Sieg was flying faster than a rumor in court.

The impact of the blow so shocking.

So ...

Spinning out of control like the gambling tops called piddly dreidels, but only by nobles who were permitted to gamble.

The trees behind the gorgeous Silke were in fact good enough to make such tops from, strange thought that, but gambling whether his luck as a Lightest One would save him from the coming thousand foot plummet ...

No!

Focus.

The wind gusting around him ...

Nothing compared to the endless air gusted by lesser nobles. The trees were just twigs to be broken. Bramble a nuisance. Boulder nothing. Moss pathetic.

A thousand foot plummet ... nothing compared to his sword.

His strength.

His determination to win.

Prove this worthless vixen wrong. Like the other lessers.

With all his might.

With breath held with perfect timing.

Sieg drove Demon Ender down.

Sliced down through boulder.

Down through rock.

Down

down

down

down

down

And twist!

Yank *ouch* to a stop. His hands holding the sword tight.

And the sword gripped the cliff tight.

But he hung off the cliff. Legs dangling off a thousand foot plummet.

Ah. Stay. Calm.

His heart dared race anyway.

No.

Stay. Calm. He was the High Prince.

And a Chosen One.

His arms were more than strong from bouts against Rowan and his ridiculous strength, combined with incredible speed and endurance. Whatever Hedge Rowan used to get that much of a boost for so long ... he never spoke about it and

Sieg could never make out what limitations and restrictions that fool imposed on himself to achieve such a boost. It was beyond what a superstrength Hedge could do. Hedges could only boost strength, speed, or endurance.

Not all so intensely.

His boots had decent scales on the bottom and they gripped the side of the cliff well enough. Better than the ground above even. After this mission he'd get them replaced with even better scales.

Sieg pulled himself up quickly.

Silke giggled sultry and sinister.

"Full of maternal rage," she said, "My other halves will do you in for me, their beloved daughter."

Both fox trolls grunted. Furious. Full of an unnatural maternal rage twisted and enhanced by the vixen's magic. No doubt they were the maternal monstrosities Sieg had heard slavomancers had bred from their lycan fodder.

But rumors said the project was abandoned due to inability to control them. Their power and rage was too much.

Crack!

The stink of broken stone. The cliff couldn't take the weight of two trolls either.

Leveraging his sword, Sieg climbed up the side of the cliff.

Just as Silke shot a bolt of blue lightning his way.

But Sieg stood firm. At the edge of the cliff.

The thousand foot plummet right behind him.

No retreat.

Never.

The plummet to his back — exactly what he needed to push forward.

The sunset to his back. The reminder of the cherry sundae awaiting his return.

Not a sign of other reinforcements from the bramble-shaped forest behind Silke as she stood tall and sinister on the tallest boulder.

Her gorgeous form against that murky back drop made Sieg ache in ways he was loath to admit openly. Enough that she deserved to die just for that. That Rowan and Razz struck right on their perverted comments.

Sieg smirked anyway.

Silently.

Stoically.

A second sheath for Demon Ender would be good. Better than any gift some lesser kingdom would offer him. His current one was better than any other he could of had made.

Silke's pelt truly made for a quality ingredient.

In a way, her beauty was entirely fur deep.

The forest and pyramid behind him could wait for now. Making Silke talk ... getting stunningly gorgeous girls to blabber their brains out to him ... a special skill only the most noble of men radiated, radiate like a sun over a forest of gorgeous women, each trying to stand out like that pathetic vixen, trying to pointless prove they weren't just another pretty tree in the massive forest to use and toss.

Rowan could deal with the demon spiders infesting the forest on the bottom of the cliff. Sieg had the most pleasing job of ridding the world of one more darkling vixen witch.

After she blabbered her brains out to him.

But first, the bolt of blue lightning.

It cracked through the freezing air.

Shot right at him.

Split and forked in countless ways. Like the chats of countless courtiers back home.

But smelling and tasting like fresh snow and ice.

Frosting Sieg's valiant face once again.

The lightning arcing around the vixen trolls.

Around the many boulders and slippery moss.

Till Demon Ender absorbed her bolt.

"Delicious," said Demon Ender, "Send more!"

And she did.

Plenty.

All consumed by Demon Ender.

"Nice try," Sieg said, "But too pathetic for words. Your regeneration isn't quite what it's cut up to be, but facing demented trolls is better than two more vixen witches."

"So you zeenk," Silke said and winked at him.

That atrocious zeenk for think ... as if she were a human from Fiona Shar.

But Rowan would of won another bet — slicing lycan in half does sometimes create multiple lycan, but since Rowan wasn't here ... he needn't to know.

Silke sent a flurry of lightning his way.

All absorbed.

Strange.

None of the lightning struck the vixen trolls. It arced to avoid them. The trolls moved forward too cautiously.

Their massive claws ...

CRACK!

CRACK!

CRACK!

The moss had iced over slightly. Making it even more slippery.

The smell of fresh snow and ice ... Sieg forced a smile.

Not a grimace.

Silke laughed again. Squealed like a terrified child.

"Now protect me, my mommies!" Snow cried.

Her fur coat wasn't the slightest bit haggard yet. She had plenty of magic left. A true vixen witch.

Wolves howled below.

And the vixen trolls launched a mama-enraged massacre of an attack.

FIFTEEN

S liding — ouch — off the spider, Roo drew his other saber dagger. Quickly finished off the few orcs the spider only crippled.

So counting on the protection of dying stabby orcs and his own dragon scale, Roo sheathed his saber daggers. Noted the closest oak trunks were a good solid *loooong* dash away.

Sure, if he used his Vorshaya speed burst, but no.

His burst skills better remain secret.

Unused for now.

The soggy ground, not the best for a quick dash. The musty smell ...

Mustier? Down here? Why ... okay, later. Stomach growling, out of place, but okay stop growling and he'd find a big juicy beast to roast au jus, using the few cooking things he had stuffed in his pouch meant for celebrating his timely victory — good.

Growl. Okay.

Treaty of Grumbling Tummy agreed upon. Now to live long enough to fulfill it.

Both tigresses hesitated. Below their knees their legs were like the hind legs of a house cat. Good for deadly pouncing. But they were basically bare in the fur so all these twitching orcs with their twitching blades — ha!

No point feeling sorry for the vile furballs. The only reason they looked fabulous rather than deformed hideous monstrosities was because that made them great to pelt, especially with their regenerative abilities and all — never mind it wasn't just darklings who breed them for it.

And around their slim necks ... collars ... ah, yes.

Thin gray collars that blended far too well their tigresses' pelts. A heart of shiny cold iron locked it snug to their necks.

And a crazier idea began to form in his head.

Again.

And a promise was a promise, even if it over losing a bet after a few too many drinks of rather decent but all-too-rare rum aptly called Dead Man's Run.

So Roo drew his revolver crossbow.

The felines both covered their chests with their claw weapons. Crouched. Backing away slowly.

Smart.

But not smart enough. The nearest trunks for cover were still a few far too many sprints away.

He walked closer.

And closer.

Orc blade banging his boot here.

Then there.

Making both tigresses twitch.

Twitch.

Bang. Twitch.

Bang. Twitch.

He aimed at Boob Eyes.

Bang. Twitch.

Bang. Twitch.

Bang. Click click — two shots at Ditz.

One hit her claws.

The other her neck. Right below her maw.

She gagged. Sliced at her neck with her own claw weapons.

But froze midway. Her collar's defensive mechanism. No lycan could slice off their collar.

Their own or others.

So she collapsed. Thrashing. The usual agony of a lycan virgin to the touch of cold silver.

Boob Eyes yowled. "Stop picking on her!"

And charged at him.

Through the dying orcs.

Started stumbling quickly. Getting slashed in the leg.

By her own dying orcs.

Roo dashed in.

She vanished? Shit.

A telejump.

Pain jabbed his back *hard*.

Then the backs of his knees. The ankles of his feet.

His dragon scale saving him.

But that screech of metal to scale. That biting burnt metal stink.

Not saved for long.

Her power — pow.

His back ribs fractured. Ouch.

Roo forced a swerve around

Blink.

Boob Eyes vanished again.

One instant — the tap of claw against the top of his cowl.

Next instant he stopped holding back.

Dodged the down thrust. One that would of broken his skull.

And the one for his neck.

Stomped on her bare paw foot.

Crunch. Into a small bloody crater.

She yowled.

Roo flung a steel stake at her head point blank.

Exploded her head.

It regenerated. The gore turning to ash.

But he flung point blank another at her chest.

Boom.

A massive hole. Gore turning to ash.

Her regeneration still fast and furious. Her body wobbling backwards.

Roo shot her in the neck. At the lock. Which ripped through her neck.

Taking off the collar.

Dropping onto the ground a good distance behind her. One ruined arrow too.

Damn it.

Then it struck —a backlash counterattack so over-whelming dark and sweltering the pressure could of erased him if not the heat alone.

Just as the Ditz struggled back to her ditzy feet.

Time to gamble. Big time.

Roo shot her collar off — through her neck.

Sending her back down.

And the pressure vanished!

No need for his Hedge — yet.

Even with both tigresses up and only a few good paces away. Fur and body recovered but a good bit ragged.

"Shit," Boob Eyes said, "He killed all our orcs and nearly got us too. Sorry Grendel, Master is going to be *so* angry with us ... we'll definitely get pelted unless we slaughter him good."

"I-I-I-I don't ... know," Platinum Ditz said, "Master i-i-i-i-is always angry. Maybe we should ... um ... Grendel?"

Grendel? Who ...

A wolf lycan growled right by the tigresses. A massive monster of a wolf lycan.

That must be Grendel.

"A strength Hedge," Grendel said, "Your knives will be of little use here. Go help finish off that elf. Her arrows could prove a nuisance."

The tigresses hesitated again.

Then vanished.

Leena could deal with them. She was a skilled knight after all.

Roo cracked his knuckles. "Let's —"

A trio of identical black wolves arrived on blacker identical spiders.

"Let us warm up on this human," they all said.

Together?

Grendel smirked. "Go ahead. His strength Hedge ... do not hold back. Use your own Hedge right away."

Those sinister identical chuckles ...

Roo knew he needed to think quick.

Or he'd die even quicker.

CHAPTER

SIXTEEN

In one. slow. instant. the mama trolls roared at Sieg. Shaking the ledge. The trees behind Silke. Rattling the bramble. Echoing throughout the valley. Echo. echo. echoing even louder. and louder. The tension of that very moment made Sieg grip his sword very tight. His dragon scale no protection. The vanishing light ... too symbolic.

The mama trolls charged at Sieg.

Smashing boulders.

Vaporizing moss.

Crack.

Crack.

Crack.

Sieg howled too. "For the Light!"

And lunged.

Hacked.

Dodged.

Sliced.

Connected — and the mama troll got sucked into the sword? Darklings didn't ...

"A delicious meal!" said Demon Ender.

A blue bolt forked at him.

Sieg dodged.

"More I say," said Demon Ender.

The other mama troll bellowed. Attacked full force.

But Sieg didn't dodge. He met the attack head on.

Slash overhead.

And the other mama troll got sucked in too.

"Delicious beyond words," said Demon Ender.

He smirked at Silke. "Another magical trick, ey?"

But now ... two snow vixens on that boulder?

Mirror image twins in stunningly beauty, so beautiful his legs almost trembled. Almost.

Their welcoming pose was so sultry the best dancers could learn from them. It was as if they were courtesans putting on some sexy show, even in that blue ice bikini armor and claws.

If there had been peace between their kinds ...

"I am Silke," the vixen to the left said.

"And I am Azura," the vixen to the right said.

Figures. Pathetic attempt at the same trick.

Azura even grinned like some dainty happy fool. Inbreed stupid, no doubt.

"You mean were," Sieg said, "Now you're both Snow."

Demon Ender laughed. "And worthy darkling flesh to wrench apart."

But vixens loved sneaky tricks, whether two footed or four, but that last quip made Silke cringe.

Azura actually giggled. So strangely happy. Stupidly happy.

"But Snow is zuch a pretty name too, no?" she said, "I like it sooo much better 💔 Vee are zee Snow twins ❣ Time to blizzard your evil butt to ice💔"

She even giggled again. Ugh. So gut wrenchingly … but honey hid poison better than vinegar, as his late uncle discovered too late, so Sieg saluted Azura for her bravo.

"It will be a pleasure," Sieg said, "To slice your stunningly gorgeous hind off and wear your tail as a scarf."

Azura stroked her tail with a naughty smirk.

"And such a cozy scarf …" she said, "It won't be 💔"

And a ball of blue flame popped up above the tip of her tail.

The smell of a fresh snow, a fresh blizzard suddenly in the air … like the mountains they had to travel through to get here.

Another vixen witch? Or a hedgie? With twins … you never know. Maybe a third trick conditioned on something united between them, no, definitely a third trick.

"Watch out Azura," Silke said, "He is more dangerous zhan —"

"I know, I know," Silva said, "But *soooo* handsome … pity, no?"

Sieg charged. "Same to you."

"So you fake flirt now?" Silke said and blasted him with more blue bolts.

Joined by the bolts her mirror twin Azura.

"I don't mind," Azura said but gave her bolts some extra blue flame.

Like her tail's flame.

Demon Ender absorbed them all. Like a drunk Rowan downing a keg, they barely slowed him down. His dragon scale boots didn't slide back.

Much.

Demon Ender laughed. "More I say! more!"

"A pretty girl is a pretty girl," Sieg said, "Let's enjoy ending them together."

"Agreed!" said Demon Ender.

But the bolts jolted his stride. Unsteadied him. Prevented any good leap.

Or thrust.

"Sieg!" said Demon Ender, "Remember Cessler's wisdom!"

Ah yes. As his swordmaster instructor Cessler the Bearded Raze battered into him again and again — don't be the trout guided by a stream, be the hawk diving for the trout.

Instead of fighting the bolt's jolts Sieg studied the forks. Calm and steady. Wound like a spring.

Let the jolts move him forward.

Not startle him.

And he rushed faster.

Faster.

Around mossy rocks. Crunching soggy frosted ground.

"Ooo, *goood* one 🖤" Azura said, "He figured zat part out. Yay 🌷 He's not all looks after all 🖤"

"Don't cheer the enemy," Silke said, "Zees is not a game."

"But I vant him even more now 🩶" Azura said, "La-sigh."

La-sigh? Oh dear Light …

"And I yearn to taste that vixen's flesh and blood," said Demon Ender.

"I am quite tasty, no?" Azura said and wiggled her furry ass at them, and … what a good ass.

But their bolts came more furious. More forked.

More unpredictable.

Sieg became more like a trout in the rapids. Crashing against mossy stone. His dragon scale saving him.

Until he slipped.

Slid into a boulder.

Started to topple — no!

He plunged Demon Ender into the ground. The blue bolts followed the blade into the ground. Crackling.

"Zee end already?" Azura said, "La-sigh 💔"

Silke growled. "Don't lower your guard!"

Demon Ender sputtered out garbled nonsense, but Sieg caught the message.

Smirked.

Yanked out his cold silver dagger. Sliced through the blue lightning.

Instantly, the bolts backlashed against Azura. Engulfing her. Shocking her. Her scream was a fiddle tune racing to his ears. The smell of burnt fox girl …

Silke grabbed her twin. She got shocked too.

But the backlash suddenly ended.

They both regenerated quickly.

Not even a hint of blood or burn fouled their white fur.

But Azura looked tired. Her fur coat ruffled. No longer so neat and trim. Silke too but not quite as much.

Azura la-sighed with a giggle and smirk?

"Zat was shockingly cold 🖤 " she said, "*Niiice* counter, blonde, but don't think you've von me over yet."

Silke tsked. "He hates us, sis, I—"

"Remember mother's advice?" Azura said, "Bitter poison doesn't get swallowed, no?"

Silke sighed.

Laughed.

"How could I forget?" Silke said, "Vee are elf girl gorgeous for a reason."

"Exactly ❣ " Azura said, "And not brainless orcs either."

Sieg saluted them again.

"And you both will make wonderful pelts," he said, "Unlike those filthy orcs."

They winked. "The best! *If* you can pelt us ..."

CRACK

From within the ledge?

"Bingo," Silke said.

Azura giggled. "As they said, no?"

Then slashed Twin Sight Slicers at him.

No. At his feet.

Missing.

But shattering the ledge.

CHAPTER

SEVENTEEN

Now Roo knew wolf lycan loved to hunt in packs. Packs of wolves. Cooperative packs.

Not the typical kitty guy, kill each other till only the strongest male lives stuff either.

That was the reason guy lycan were breed to be wolves and not tigers, lions, or other felines. Sometimes the wolves got tigresses to join but few tigresses did, thankfully, because tigresses always were leery around male of their kind, even though it was only wolves nowadays, all because of the brutal legacy of male feline lycan.

(According to the knights.)

(See he did listen to lectures, despite what everyone seemed to think.)

But first this trio of dark wolves.

The mat of dying jabby orcs banging his boots didn't even prod the wolves at all, and none of the spiderweb-shaped trees and their toupees of leaves, let alone their winding thick trunks, well, none of them were nearby. Nope. They were all a good many paces away. So no cover. Not any hope of any.

Good.

Even with plenty of branches well above him, Good to encourage the obvious ambush — as long as he didn't get careless.

Leena was still fighting the flea knights and now the tigresses were headed over to team up on her. Razz should already be ready to help her out.

Time to finish things up here and quick.

So Roo sighed. "One against three ..."

All three wolves laughed.

Until Roo added, "Trying to even those odds."

"Even?!" they all growled together.

Yes. Together.

Far too well timed.

"Nice try but ..." Roo said, "Let's even them up even more."

He put away his revolver crossbow. Snapped some straps over his other weapons.

Each and every one of them.

"See?" Roo said, "One unarmed knight. I'd undress too, but that'll take too long."

That got the three snarling fierce.

All together too. Perfectly timed.

"All three of you," Roo said, "Come. At once. I don't have all day."

The three all lunged howling.

Till Grendel snarled, "WAIT! Your Hedge!"

But too late.

Roo quickdrew.

Fired his revolver.

A bolt right into the nearest's open maw. Into its brain.

Killing all three at once.

Grendel snarled. "Tytus! Come! We—"

When a thick deep BOOOOOM rang out.

From the direction of the pyramid.

Which was nothing compared to what came next.

EIGHTEEN

It cost Leena one of her sungwood daggers ... but the flea knights were destroyed.

That wonderful smell of moss, yes, it warmed her more than the sun itself. It awakened a pride that the stink of dead exploded flea couldn't dampen. A relief sweeter than a lemonade cool and fresh after that last hiking over a volcano for endurance training months ago.

Her dragon scale fit nice and snug. Stretched with her breathing just find, unlike those horrible corsets human women insisted on wearing. Her body felt just as fresh now.

For a moment.

Until the sweat making her stink like some fruity desert damped her pride a bit.

And the scratch of moss dusting her insides reminded her of the price of victory.

The thick branch had sustained serious damage too. The

bark was all but gone. Craters in the wood. The dangerously loud creaks ... the shifting shadows by the spiderwebs and leaves ... demon spiders torn between instincts to flee and instincts to wait and ambush.

The flea tigress ... ah. Right above her.

Ready to pounce. Her orange fur more than visible from the branch twisting above the one Leena was on.

Leena summoned her bow of light.

Drew an arrow of light.

She could only fire as many arrows as she had spent in the light for her whole life. Every hour in the light gave her one more arrow she could use once thereafter.

No need for a quiver.

In return for this Hedge the only other major limitation was that she could no longer wield a different bow and arrow, let alone a regular one. So once she ran out of arrows, she had to spend hours in the light to get more arrows. Spend as much time in the sun to gain as many arrows as she could when she would need them.

A terrible limitation during a drawn out battle between large factions.

But here, not so bad.

The black-haired tigress hissed.

"Such a cute moss Hedge," she said, "Too bad I'll never—"

She flung a block iron dagger at Leena's face.

Leena sidestepped quick.

Thunk!

Two more daggers coming. So close together.

Leena sidestepped back. Around the other dagger.

Her dragon scale should protect her from any brief deadly brush of the dark metal.

CLACK!

The daggers collided midair?!

One flew right at her face.

So fast.

Leena ducked.

Backwards.

It ripped her cowl off. Cloak off too.

Threw off her balance.

But Leena jerked forward. Knee slamming the branch.

The loud creak and shake — the branch would soon fall.

But her balance was back.

Her head was fully exposed now. Her neck-length blond hair was a mess. Blocked the edge of her vision. Worse than the double wedge hairdo her little sister insisted on Leena having off duty.

Risking a talk Hedge trap but ...

"Amazing trick," Leena said, "I'd—"

The tigress laughed. "Enjoy seconds then!"

Another pair of daggers came down fast.

Both so close to each other. Same trick.

Leena sidestepped — ack!

Tripped over the first dagger she had dodged. Fell onto her side.

CLACK!

Right at her face!

She rolled. Aimed.

Twang!

Boom.

The arrow destroyed the incoming dagger utterly.

Leena drew another arrow. "Now your turn tig—"

The tigress was no longer above her.

But two pairs of daggers were headed her way. Roll up and she'll die. Stay down and she'll die.

Unless ... twang. twang.

Daggers blown away.

Leena rolled up. The branch sunk deeper than it should of.

Felt lighter.

She ducked. Turning around.

Orange striped black!

The tigress had telejumped right behind her. Was now jabbing where Leena's head had been a moment earlier. With black iron claw extenders.

Leena fired. "Good try."

The arrow blew away the tigress' entire chest. Much of its shoulder belt and daggers too. Shoved the body back.

She regenerated quick.

But the tigress was already on her knees.

Claw extenders dug into the branch.

"Meow to come," the tigress said and slipped out of the claw extenders.

Punning meow for more? *Ugh.*

"Then hurry," Leena said and blasted away the tigress' chest again.

The tigress gasped something before her chest regenerated.

So Leena blasted her head away.

Then her chest.

The regenerating body flew back. Her fur so haggard only a shot or two should be needed now.

No need to use another arrow.

Leena yanked out her last sungwood dagger.

Lunged to plunge the tip through the cat's heart. Paralyze it.

But the tigress vanished.

Telejumped.

Careless fool she was Leena — ack!

She swerved around.

Ducked.

A cold iron dagger swooshed right over her ear.

CLANK!

And into her neck.

CHAPTER

NINETEEN

The whole world shook as if Roo fell into another empty keg falling down another set of spiraling stairs.

No.

Wait.

He *was* in a keg. Somehow. There *was* wood around. Somehow. Wood planks were bent around him. Him curled up. Stuffed in the keg. The familiar smell of ale bruising his nose. His head pounding harder than the bangs shaking the keg regularly. Wood hitting wood. Rolling it faster. Flipping it faster. And faster. And faster. And wood hitting stone—

Screams from nearby? Screams and death cries!

Cries that elves were attacking. Slaughtering everyone.

He had to — no. Wait.

His dragon scale was gone?!

What the ...

He was bare in the ... his breath more shallow than a vixen's looks. He was colder than a vixen's heart. More bruised than ... than ...

No!

There was something between him and the wood. Thick yet short. His mouth. His nose. All felt ... bigger. Teeth. Sharper.

His hands smother his face. Hands that ... furry? A mouth and nose that ... a cat's maw!

Not a wolf, but a cat ... orange with stripes like his own mother? Not a wolf but a — oh crap.

He roared.

Roared like a tiger denied him his beloved catnip-flavored ale.

The smell of elf ... like a bowl of fruit-punch spiked with liquor heaven.

He tried to move, but no, the keg didn't budge. Just kept rolling. Banging and banging. Banging him more and more.

Until he struggled to stay conscious.

A struggle he'd soon lose.

Unless ... he had no choice.

Roo triggered his Hedge.

And everything vanished.

Sucked into a black hole in his chest.

And what remained shocked Roo to the core.

TWENTY

Thank the Light Sieg never revealed his Hedge.

Between him and the jagged boulders a thousand feet below — nothing but the falling rubble of the ledge.

That awful stink of broken rock, too much like how the finest masons should smell, and once this disaster was dealt with, he'd send a troupe of masons here to build a proper city out of this place.

And the sun almost set.

Good.

The ledge was all gone. Nothing between him and the boulder those two vixens Silke and Azura stood triumphantly on.

Bare in the fur except for their pale blue collars.

Even the forest behind them ... it was too murky now to even show its bramble form.

Until Sieg triggered his Hedge.

He burst into a ball of flames. Flame of the whitest, purest light. Lit this awful forest brighter than the noon sun could ever hope to.

Both Silke and Azure gasped together.

But Azura spoke first, "Aaaah 🖤 *So* beautiful ❣ "

And her big bright eyed gaze at him. Like blue lightning shocking her—

No.

She needed to die first.

Before—

Silke giggled sinister. "Maybe vee should—"

Azura bounced in place. "Yes ❣ *Yes* ❣ **Yes** ❣ He must die before vee do. Sorrrrriiiieee 💔 "

"Apologize to your darkness," Sieg said, "For failing it so badly!"

And he flew at them.

Roasting away the falling stone in his way.

Sizzling away the moss. Like the stink of Leena and her silly Hedge.

Yet Azura Azure only grinned whiter at him.

At his coming to kill her.

"My final request to you is ..." she said.

He refused to take her bait. His flames reached for her and her beautiful twin.

Ready to burn their evil hinds to—

They transformed into glassy ice ... no. They weren't cold. They didn't melt. Didn't smell of ice. They — no!

Diamonds?!

He tried to jerk back his flames.

But it was too late.

Azure grabbed it with her diamond hand.

And sucked him in.

before he realized it, he was just a little orb within her chest. Like a little glowing white heart.

"One Chosen down 🤍" she said, "And One more to go ❣️"

And there was nothing Sieg could do about it.

For now.

CHAPTER

TWENTY-ONE

Roo woke up among the dying orcs. His heart racing at a sight he couldn't remember, and prayed he wouldn't anytime soon.

Yet he couldn't help but stare up into those familiar spiderwebbish trees with leafy toupees webbed all over them and ah!

So much like those drawings his mother loved to tease him with way back when ... yes, those secret kitty cat things she used her Hedge to make him forget.

So he wouldn't reveal his own half-blood carelessly.

He wouldn't hesitate to protect himself against furred kin that would seek to kill him no matter what.

And this forest still smelled mustier than all the abandoned cedars, wells, and whatnot his mother dragged him to furred study ancient whatnot, yet unlike those places, not a mess in sight.

Yet Roo gulped at what he saw next.

Shocked to the core.

Several paces away. On the ground. Leena. Cowl down. A stake through her throat. Gagging. Dying.

That wolf lycan Grendel had already ripped off her dragon scale.

Ripped off his own ... and his wolfhood was already ready to ... while Leena and her gorgeous legs were being spread and ... that the last thing she'd ...

Roo roared.

Triggered a full speed burst.

Power burst.

And one punch from behind. Slammed Grendel into bloody gore splattered some tree.

A giant spider howled behind Roo — and then died next.

Leena gagged. Sputtering blood from her mouth.

"R-r-roo?" she said.

"I ... I'm sorry. I ..." he said, and removed his cowl and cloak. Covered her body with it quick but tender.

"Please ..." she said, "Take it out and ..."

She shut her eyes ... changing ... into an orange tigress?!

Roo gulped again. "Alright."

And he ripped the stake from her throat. Her throat recovered quick?

Reaching for his hand, Leena purred. "Nice save, but we're not done yet. If Sieg ..."

A sinister cackle rang out behind them

"Sieg is dead, sweeties 🤍" a girl said, "And soon you traitors will be too — AH!"

A boom erupted near the newcomer.

A huff from above them?

The light thumps behind him. The smell of the three tigresses from before ...

A smell of lustful kitty girl delight?!

TWENTY-TWO

Even with his heart pounding lustful stupid, somehow Roo managed to turn around quick.

Note how the murk turned even murkier.

The smell even mustier.

And utter silence beyond the few right by him.

Even the dying orcs were dead silent now.

The spiderwebbish trees seemed to curl in closer. Their leafy toupees seemed to have even more webs weaving them together.

Yet glowing bright in the murk was a pair of drop dead gorgeous snow vixens.

And the three tigresses he had been fighting were now standing before him. As if protecting him from the vixens?

Sexy Stripes giggled sultry. Rubbing her own neck.

"No collar," she said, "No listen."

Boob Eyes joined with the giggle. "Sooo much easier to breath too."

Platinum Ditz took such a deep breath, yikes.

"And use our best Hedges!" she said.

BOOOM!

Ditz ... had drawn a bow of light, had fired an arrow of light at the vixens.

"Return to your masters," Ditz said, "And—"

Both vixens laughed. Unharmed?

"Our foxling race has revived ❣ " one said, "And once I absorb Sieg, I shall be the finest Chosen ever ❣ "

The other sneered. "Zee victory is ours, no?"

Roo chuckled, smirking just as sinister at both of them.

"No," he said, "It's time to use *my* hedge."

He reached within himself. His fingers against his chest. Against his heart.

And pulled out a black hole.

TWENTY-THREE

The black hole was darker than any abyss, magical or not. The murk of these woods seemed bright compared to it. It very smell, an absence so stark, it was like his nose broke. His taste vanished.

His hearing dimmed. As if any sound had to pierce a thick pillow of nothing.

But this black swirling ball of nothingness, it was the loss of hope for his enemies, and so it's size, at first, the size of a seer's crystal ball, nearly as big as his own chest, yet it's weight, he could only hope to move it through magic, and its hungry, anything that Roo wished to feed it.

Even both of those vixens.

Their magic.

Both gasped.

"No! It's not fair," one of them said, "We won. We won. We'd finally not be alone!"

"Zee world," the other vixen said, "is not fair, Silke, no?"

The vixen with an accent ripped a bright glowing orb out of her chest. The voice coming from out of the orb …

It was Roo's turn to gasp.

"Sieg?" Roo said, "Weird hedge you have there …"

The accented vixen smirked. "But a gift you earned, no?"

And she flung the orb at Roo's black hole.

The Sieg-orb flew right at the black hole.

With all his magic, Roo yanked the black hole out of the way just in time.

But the Sieg-orb got flung far away.

But safe.

When out of the darkness it came.

From the black hole!

The humanoid creature was wrapped in a dark cloak. Floating like a sinister phantom of shadow and green magical mist. With a crown of thorns over its hooded cowl. Smelling of death and a toxic burning potion of unknown contents.

A slavomancer.

The accented vixen gasped.

"But zee traitors …" she said, "Vee … zee humans turned to foxlings, no?"

It hissed. "Kneel, or *die.*"

The vixens fell. Kneeling so deep they were practically lying face down, and trembling. their terrified stink strong even from several paces away.

Roo growled. "What humans? Where—"

The slavomancer chuckled.

"A few pathetic tigresses for a village of humans," it said,

"Humans that seeded the revival of the foxling race. Enjoy your little harem. We shall claim your young when it is time."

It extended a skeletal dark hand out.

And the vixens vanished.

Along with the slavomancer.

TWENTY-FOUR

The spiderwebbish trees seemed to curl away from Sieg, from his whole body, as it glowing a bright light, almost as bright as the sun, except without the burning glare and after spots in your vision.

Roo forced himself to blink.

Then again.

The trees' leafy toupees seemed to have fewer webs weaving through them now, and even the many, many spiders seemed to back away. Flee from the light.

Their hisses and creaks echoed from the countless shadows. Shadows hungry to retake this land.

The dark dank soil seemed drier now. More earthy rather than musty. A normal deep dark forest with craggy trees making a woody cathedral meant for deer and squirrels, not overgrown spiders.

Hint of ferns were already budding out of the soul by Sieg's feet.

How about that? Really.

Bracken was really needed here, of all places. Made the place less ... murky. Less spooky. More beautiful.

Some of the ferns even touched a brave hangry spider and ... oh my ... *wow*.

It curled into a spiderly ball. Squealing like the mice it so definitely loved to feast on, and shuttered.

Then went pop!

And out came a ... fairy?

Yeah.

A three-inch high blonde with lush shoulder length hair, blue swallowtail wings and fluffy white antenna. her giggle was as sweet as Leena's, and her light made even more spiders hiss hangry and furious.

"Sieg's a ..." Roo said.

"Enough," Sieg said.

But it clearly wasn't.

More and more of the spiders squealed into spidery balls. Went pop!

More fairies.

Mostly beautiful girls but ...

Roo sighed. "No wonder you're so popular with the ladies."

All the newborn fairies giggled.

Sieg simply grumbled. "With that furball form ... I still recognize you ... and ..."

Silence, except for more squealing spiders.

"If you tell anyone ..." he said.

Roo could only smirk. "I won't tell anyone ... because I'll tell everyone."

"Fairies ..." Sieg said, "Inflict *that* curse on him ..."

They all giggled sinister.

The first fairy snickering the cutest, zipped right over in front of Roo, and said, "I'm Peaches. I'll be your greatest love in another world that—"

"Ha!" Roo said, "Another world ... why should I care?"

"The worlds are connected," she said, "And now we are. You'll seeeeeeeeee — he-he."

"I can't wait ..." Roo said.

But the flutter of his heart at this ... Peaches now ...

Roo managed to snort. "We'll see."

"Yup," Peaches said, "More than see — he-he."

"I'll leave you and your little fairies alone," Roo said, "Just make sure you don't leave any spiders or else all these poor helpless fairies ..."

Sieg snorted. "I know my duty. Do you know yours?"

Roo refused to dignify that with a response.

CHAPTER

TWENTY-FIVE

The sunrise was a cherry custard for the eyes, and a sunrise on a new day for mankind.

Especially back on top of this thousand foot cliff.

The pyramid was gone. Vanished.

No sign of it.

Just like the squeals and cries were all of spiders and worse being hatched into fairies and more annoying stuff best not faced for no reason.

The spiderwebbish trees and their leafy toupees could be explored another day.

When Roo had better control over his newly discovered form.

(Mother sure had some explaining to do.)

Since, sure, climbing a thousand foot cliff was far easier

as a tiger guy than as a human guy, even if all four tigresses enjoy every slip and slide he took on the way up.

(Sieg could find his own way up.)

At least his gamble paid off. His mother wasn't the only tigress who yearned for more than what the slavomancers offered.

And the lustful scents suggested they were ... open to the notion of ... helping him restore the Vorshaya clan.

Okay.

Having a bunch of cublings right now ... yeah, they were more than just open, but not here, not now.

Even Leena.

Who seemed to think her elf kind would accept the newly freed tigresses. That more than a few elves of her homeland were now mixed blood with lycan that they could find elf boy wolves willing and eager to girlfriend them.

She even suggested he come with her.

At least they both were back in their dragon scale. Fur wasn't as great against the elements here as Roo thought it would be.

But after a night of snuggling with sultry tigresses ... well, Roo could understand both his fathers better now.

Especially now, when he took Leena's hand, and she suddenly put it over her breast.

And she smiled. "You'll do anything for me now, right?"

His cheeks. So hot. her chest. So soft.

"Of course," he said.

She laughed. "Just as I thought."

And she leaned in, and gave him a nice quick kiss.

"In my elf form ..." she said, and stopped?

Just like last night.

"Helpless after sex," Roo said.

"How'd you know?" Leena said.

"My mother ..." he said, "Is a scholar, of sorts."

"Then your father ..." she said, and that glare of hers.

"Nonono," he said, "She's a tigress too."

That got him a gasp.

"How ..." she said.

"It's a long story," he said.

"And we have a long journey ahead of us," Leena said.

And she added with a smile. "And four cute tigresses eager to know you better too."

Then pressed his hand against her chest again.

"You know my weakness way too well," he said.

She kissed him again, and this time, with more than a long wet purr.

ABOUT THE AUTHOR

Widely traveled, Jonathan Evan Hudson spends as much time studying life as he does writing gripping tales of fantastic adventures. From the giant redwoods of California to the deserts of Israel, his thrilling stories all draw on first-hand experiences and expand them with the fantastic and his acclaimed creativity.

Be the first to know!
For the updates and more:
www.JonathanEvanHudson.com

youtube.com/@jonathanevanhudson
tiktok.com/@jonathan.evan.hudson

A War Of Lust And Oak

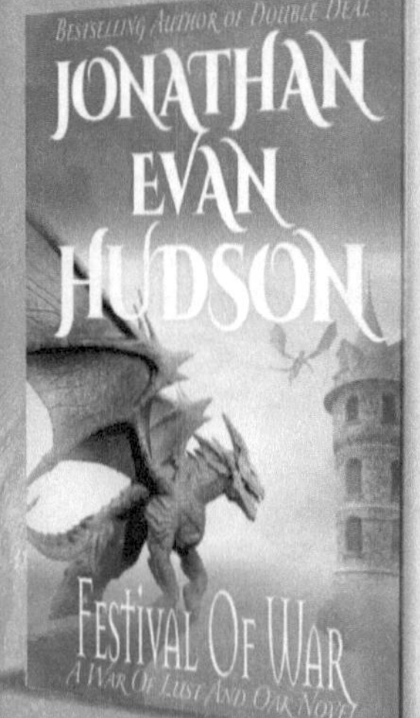

Read Now!

The Elf Girl Effect

The acclaimed Jonathan Evan Hudson once again weaves an unforgettable tale brimming with spicy page-turning action and fast-burning enemies-to-lovers passion.

Meet the newly knighted Roo Vorshaya. Sworn to protect humanity in the isolated mountain town of Appleharth. Dreams of action-packed adventure and passionate love under a lovely but sinister strawberry-pink sky.

Love re-ignited by a whiff of the familiar peaches and cream scent of his long-lost childhood girlfriend: the notorious elven witch Amber Peaches.

And endangering everything Roo holds dear.

Love page-turner novels of epic fantasy? Love reading from dusk to dawn? Then go read *The Elf Girl Effect* now!

Martial Art Of The Phantom Saber

Read Now!

Succubus Slash

The acclaimed Jonathan Evan Hudson weaves an unforgettable tale of thrilling action and adventure spiced with fast-burning romance and doused deep in epic fantasy.

Enter Miles Mayhem. Rich in friends and enemies. And a fat boy badass in the sword.

A seriously delicious smell of bacon and eggs smothered in spiced razor-hot cheddar signals celebration—and serious trouble ahead.

Trouble beyond anything Miles ever expected.

The perfect epic fantasy novel. A genre-enlarging feast for fans of sexy action and fabulous adventure. Read *Succubus Slash* now!

Sword Master Of Honey Heart Resort

Read Now!

Into Shadow Forest

Read Now!

A diamond in the rough the bestselling Jonathan Evan Hudson weaves a thrilling tale from explosive beginning to satisfying end in the awe-inspiring land of Grandcrest.

The talented twenty-something sword master Romeo Bladell yearns for love and adventure.

And at the musty edges of Shadow Forest. Near the towering high oaks bearded like stout old dwarves. By a canyon like a wound gnashed deep through in the granite. A canyon like the maw of a stone dragon.

A strange unexpected rope bridge hangs silently. Sinisterly.

Beckoning adventure—and danger unimaginable.

Enter *Into Shadow Forest* and savor the most spectacular of page-turning epic fantasy novels. Love unique monsters, riveting battles, and fantastic femme fatales? Then read *Into Shadow Forest* now!

Angels Of The Sword

Read Now!

Crossing Of Shadowed Death

Read Now!

The acclaimed master of fantasy Jonathan Evan Hudson once again shines through with his talented story-telling. Time to enter another stunning awe-inspiring world of dangerous demons, magical mayhem, and action-packed adventure.

A simple demon-hunting mission. The young and lonely Dirk yearns for amazing adventure, for gorgeously under-dressed dancer girls among the towering high ferns. Among the even taller pines of the hot and humid Fern Shadow Forest.

Pine needles everywhere. And so fragrant they made the finest of teas.

Sturdy reliable cobble roads of the Divine Empire cut through the whole entire forest. Providing the only safe passage.

Or so Dirk thought ...

Enjoy this sexy, action-packed epic fantasy adventure from the talented Jonathan Evan Hudson. Love to read an enthralling epic fantasy novel full of stunning rip-roaring battles with creative new monsters? Then go read *Crossing of Shadowed Death* now!

A TASTE OF THE ELF GIRL EFFECT

The acclaimed Jonathan Evan Hudson once again weaves an unforgettable tale brimming with spicy page-turning action and fast-burning enemies-to-lovers passion.

Meet the newly knighted Roo Vorshaya. Sworn to protect humanity in the isolated mountain town of Appleharth. Dreams of action-packed adventure and passionate love under a lovely but sinister strawberry-pink sky.

Love re-ignited by a whiff of the familiar peaches and cream scent of his long-lost childhood girlfriend: the notorious elven witch Amber Peaches.

And endangering everything Roo holds dear.

*Love page-turner novels of epic fantasy? Love reading from dusk to dawn? Then go read **The Elf Girl Effect** now!*

CHAPTER I

ROO

The sky was a strawberry custard for the eyes, and the same color of the lips Roo yearned to kiss.

So what if the clouds behind him were dark and ominous? The wind gusty and chilled more than the perfect shot of vodka. The taste of rain electrified by lightning-to-be ...

The street was as slim as his chances of success.

The cobble as bumpy as the journey ahead.

And this hill — a steep ascent into danger.

Roo even wore a jerkin woven of the finest dragon scale the son of ~~an~~ thee Exiled Exorcist of Most Notable Notoriety could hope to earn as one of the last members of the Vorshaya Clan.

Yup.

The Vorshaya clan. The once very badassed clan nearly wiped out to protect the greatest of the great Oak of Ages, a source of lightful magic and all from … something, something he'd hunt down and deal with.

Still, if his mother hadn't been doing scholarly stuff far away at the time … if she hadn't taken him with her …

Sigh.

He didn't like to think about it much.

But his jerkin was pale blue as the sky … wasn't today.

But it was one only worn by the best of the best True TriCross Knights. The big, white triple cross on his chest proclaimed it for all to see.

And a chance to pursue his dream to travel the world.

Slay monsters and save people, without any of that bounty hunter nonsense either.

Explores things, places that no one's ever explored before, or okay, more like no one's explored in living memory …

Or longer.

His jerkin, it even had the snazziest, puffiest shoulder guards of the palest, bluest cold silver, and they were so so perfectly round that a certain Motherly Scholar of Notable Nagging couldn't hope to find a single fault with.

Just like the trusty pouch she made for him.

Shaped like a chubby triple cross, it was strapped to his waist and she magicked it to hold far more than you'd think it could and weigh so much less.

And just like his pouch, his slacks were as blue as the sky … wasn't … today.

And … okay okay.

Anyways, his boots, and girls were obsessed with footwear or else the boot merchants wouldn't cater to girls so utterly much, so anyways, his boots were a snazzy dark blue suede, like the coming night sky should be (but obviously won't be. Pink sky meant severe storm coming.)

And with the coming storm …

There were even spooky tentacles of mist rising from the street, and that only happened when a serious storm was coming through.

But the not so distant rumbles … wasn't only thunder.

So not much time left …

Good thing he wore a pair of sabers and a whip. One saber was of the bluest, sharpest cold silver, and the other, the blackest, sharpest cold steel, a stronger variant of cold iron, and the whip was made of pretty strong scarlet dragon scales, with the dragon magic woven strongly within the whip.

Good for offense and defense, against magical and nonmagical trouble too.

Sort of.

As long as he didn't whip his eye out, like his mother often teased.

Even more important, his trusty arm guards were both cold silver and cold steel forged together. His left arm guard could extend into a shield. The right held a miniature bow with a string of holy blue magic so that, with the right motion flicking motion, it would fire bolts of holy blue light or unholy violet light.

Perfect for a True TriCross Knight.

His heart raced for the coming battle.

For the girl she would soon save.

Since nothing, absolutely *nothing* raced a heart like that elven fragrance, that whiff of the sweetest of peaches and cream only moments ago in this sweet sweltering hot afternoon.

No doubt about it.

The elf girl of his wildest dream come true. Right now. Here in the sexy flesh ...

Amber Peaches: a lust dream come true.

No.

Thee one and **best** lust dream come true.

And the muddy road here was a nice reminder of years ago, back when Peaches and Row got to quipping each other and their quipping got so fierce it broke out into mud wrestling that if, today their reunion broke into mud wrestling, wow, that would be so sexy amazing ...

Sniiiiiiiff.

It smelled ... surprisingly fresh. Earthy forest mud, no, soil fresh.

The lampposts at the street corners ... they were cold iron. The blackest of cold iron and forged like incredibly narrow, but tall, tulips of utter moonless midnight black.

Ah.

The oil lamps on top were those genie-style lamps to be wicked for the evening and wow, did they make the olive oil merchants rich.

But ... it was the genies inside that kept the mud clean. Kept their lamps lit at night, but what those genies were ...

Elf girls captured and lamped into genies due to the war

between humans and demons, and well, elves were demons after all, and elves were the fully evolved form of fairies.

Even Peaches.

But the rumble of distant thunder that wasn't thunder was almost louder than his own tummy rumbling for some peaches and cream pie, especially after that sexy whiff of long missed Peaches.

(All better to tease Peaches with too.)

((Sure, elves should thank the Light their natural body odor, after lots of sweaty work, was so fruity nice rather than so gut-wrenching stinky like humans, you know, like him, but either way, frequenting the public baths, a necessity, human or elf.))

(But not first date material.)

((Outside of certain smut rags kept hidden under the best lock and key in an undisclosed location.))

(((*Very* undisclosed.)))

Even now, the sun was still as blonde as Peaches' waist-long hair, so no worries.

Last they ran into each other, back before war and puberty tore them apart, her hair was ass-long but also far far messier.

Just like back then, she styled the bangs to fountain off the sides of her head like gorgeously floppy wings, plus a floppy witch hat of rosy pink, that, of course, would hide her huuuuge but adorably pointy elf ears.

Ears so long and pointy, that resembled a cross between kitty and fawn ears, especially how they always were moving about so expressively.

So all in all, he wasn't so distracted by her fine ass in a finer minidress, (and it was the ultra-short, ultra snug and stretchy kind that was like strawberry custard to the eyes, ears, and loins,) so no, in that critical moment, he didn't walk into a wall.

No.

He walked into a door.

And as the Light would have it, there was plenty of wall he could of walked into.

The stone floors of the half-timber houses all along this block. All painted as colorfully as a field of wildflowers, but full of apples, apple blossoms, and even more apples.

This town was called Appleharth for a reason.

A very good reason.

And the door he did walk into was the usual solid sturdy oak, so no worries, it took the beating well.

Sure, there was ... a crack down the middle of the door now.

Sure. From him.

But the door's paint job was still spectacular.

No clumsy clod could hope to ruin those artful swathes of banana streaks full of cherry swirls. In fact, there wasn't even a nick to show for his clumsy moment.

Other than a wide crack down the middle.

And by the hinges too.

Roo credited his snazzy cowl and mouth cloth for softening the blow. They were as pale blue as the sky ... wasn't ... today.

But they were the color of Peaches' bright blue eyes ...

well, last time they ran into each other years and years ago, over a decade ago. More than a decade ago. Wait. Same thing. Okay.

Good.

Dazed but not confused. A door would not stop him.

Or delay him.

Much.

Now one more chance or else ... he'd regret it for the rest of his life.

CHAPTER 2

PEACHES

otally fucking ... that poster of parchment ... those blocky black letters spelling WANTED ...

Oh, for the Oak of Ages ... Peaches totally fucking wanted to give the middle finger to that sly sneak of a trickster the moment she spotted that parchment poster hanging all cozy and sinister and sooo much like a little black widow on those shutters behind the windowsill of those stinkier than stinky roses.

The sky wouldn't be the only one growling soon.

Good thing Peaches wore her finger loop gloves snug and ready. Each was as scarlet red as she'd soon make that trickster, what's her face, the Rouge Reapist, and even better, there were pentacles of unicorn hair woven into each palm to speed up her magic casting faster than a fox pouncing a mouse.

Along the glove were cute heart-shaped gaps. Normally,

they'd hold rosy pink hearts, each of which held a precast spell she could fling at a target for instant effect, but she ran out a while ago and seeing a human alchemist ... pretty dangerous when her kind made such good ingredients to those sorts.

But that thunder close by, not just thunder.

The narrow street echoed the rumble and only confirmed the groan of a dire ogre coming this way.

Strange how there weren't any screams.

Disturbing, in fact.

Regular people shouldn't be so calm around one, unless ... no.

Peaches didn't want to think of it.

Yet.

It was bad enough that the pink sky, as lovely as it was, meant the coming storm would be terrible, if her father's stories held any truth to them.

(Big if.)

But no telling what these half-timber houses were hiding then. So what if they were beautifully decorated with apples, apples, and more apples? Plus a flower or two.

A chill seemed to ache her whole spine.

A warning of danger.

Demonic danger.

Nearby.

Never mind elves were technically lightspawn, a kind of demon, but of the light, so too many humans, sigh.

Least she usually could be reborn a few more times.

More than a few, actually.

Nine lives, like a cat, but three already used, but least her power and beauty were upped each time, but she started out as a brand new fairy, hatching from the Oak of Ages, and had to find another compatible human girl to fuse with, eat her soul and sigh.

No wonder some human despised demons of   all sorts.

If her brother only had one life ... if she only had one life ... like these humans ... sigh.

Why Roo even understood way back when ... sigh.

But the lamppost of black iron, horribly styled like tall and narrow tulips, no, that burn to their smell, a burn like that death pepper chili that little brat Roo tricked her stupid bratty self into trying long ago (and stupid her tried it again and again and again ...)

But it was definitely cold iron.

A quick way to a really, really awful death.

No wonder she couldn't pinpoint the source of demonic danger.

No doubt it was darkspawn demons but so what?

This was just a step toward her true dream, becoming an elf witch explorer, and discover why there's so many ruins appearing here and there, and elves had extension records proving some of these ruins appeared without a civilization before, as if it had been moved there.

Some even came from the future.

Others were from the distant past. Ruins that should no longer exist.

Ruins full of monsters.

So today, good practice.

Peaches made a point to keep strutting down the road without hesitation or obvious concern.

If orcs were hunting her ... letting them know she sensed something suspicious, especially as a witch with her fore-sense able to detect danger and ill intent toward her, well, according to her training, a big no no.

And despite it being in the early afternoon, the shutters of all the half-timber houses were shut.

Locked.

Other human towns she'd been in ... plenty of dumb human girls overlooked her demonic side and drooled over her looks, but here, today? Nope. Not one dumbass to brush off.

Something was off.

Good thing she could summon her bow and arrows of light quicker than any other elf in her generation, guy or girl. Several split seconds ahead of the best of the best guys and rapid fire better too. She could even build up plenty of blessed arrows as long as she got enough sunlight during the day, each day to build up and store more blessings for arrows for when she'd need them.

At least if any orc managed to get too close, the stiletto heels of her thigh boots could double as slyly placed daggers.

Alicorn style. Beauty and power came together for elf girls, so lucky her.

And her alicorn was the high grade spiraled kind.

Her boots were as scarlet red as she'd made those orcs.

Normally, she had rosy pink hearts lacing them snug up

her leg. They normally would hold spells she could fling off for instant magical attacks just like her gloves.

But right now, like her gloves, they were just a bunch of heart-shaped gaps.

At least her rosy pink minidress and witch hat were woven with silk of a spellbinder silkworm. They weren't protective against blade and fang, or even against magic … but they both together were a huge reserve of extra magic that naturally refilled as long as she wore them enough, especially in sunlight.

Even today.

And to fuck with the mind of those perverted orc bastards, she went with the sluttiest minidress she could manage. Translucent silk, so the right angles, the right nude elf deluxe, he-he.

So double the weirdness that no human guys went lusty dumbass toward her today.

Not even the gate guards.

Okay. Gate guards rarely did. Being a guard was all reputation and honor, not about coin. Any act tarnishing that, tarnished all the guards, and the guard loathed that.

Plus, her rosy pink minidress had the perfect distract and destroy notch down the front. One that showed far more than the little it covered.

Including her bra of ruby hearts.

And her chest, buxom to the extreme.

With only a few stretched to the breaking ruby ties down each the notches, the slutty side notches revealed more than just her tasty midriff, they revealed a good solid hint of her lace panties.

Ruby lace.

Orcs were rapeholic monsters, after all. She might as well use their lust smitten idiocy against them.

Roo would so laugh and approve.

(And leer.)

((Leer plenty.))

(((Sigh. *Boys.*)))

((((But if he didn't … her pointy tipped boots, his rear, he-he.))))

WANT MORE?

Go to

WANT MORE?

Go to

www.JonathanEvanHudson.com